OXFORD STUDENT TEXTS

Series Editor: Victor Lee

Alexander Pope
The Rape of the Lock

Edited by Elizabeth Gurr

Oxford University Press

OXFORD
UNIVERSITY PRESS

Great Clarendon Street, Oxford OX2 6DP

Oxford University Press is a department of the University of Oxford.
It furthers the University's objective of excellence in research, scholarship,
and education by publishing worldwide in

Oxford   New York

Auckland   Cape Town   Dar es Salaam   Hong Kong   Karachi
Kuala Lumpur   Madrid   Melbourne   Mexico City   Nairobi
New Delhi   Shanghai   Taipei   Toronto

With offices in

Argentina   Austria   Brazil   Chile   Czech Republic   France   Greece
Guatemala   Hungary   Italy   Japan   South Korea   Poland   Portugal
Singapore   Switzerland   Thailand   Turkey   Ukraine   Vietnam

Oxford is a registered trade mark of Oxford University Press
in the UK and in certain other countries

British Library Cataloguing in Publication Data
Data available

ISBN 978-0-19-911656-0

7 9 10 8 6

Typeset by Palimpsest Book Production Limited, Grangemouth, Stirlingshire

Printed and bound by CPI Group (UK) Ltd, Croydon, CR0 4YY

The publishers would like to thank the following for permission to reproduce
photographs: pvi: National Portrait Gallery; p79: The Victoria and Albert Museum; p81: The
British Library; p85: The Courtauld Institute of Art, Witt Library; p86: The Trustees of the
British Museum; p91, 92, 93, 94: The British Library.

Pope's letter to Arabella Fermor is reprinted from *The Correspondence of Alexander Pope*
Volume 1, edited by George Sherburn (Clarendon Press, 1956), by permission of
Oxford University Press.

Artwork is by Martin Cottam, p80.

Contents

✔ KU-539-143

Acknowledgements

The text of this edition was first published by OUP in 1966, edited by J.S. Cunningham. I have followed his edition, I hope faithfully, and I record here my thanks. His edition derived principally from the great Twickenham edition by Geoffrey Tillotson to whose meticulous scholarship all subsequent Pope editors are deeply indebted.

It will be apparent from the Notes and Interpretations that the work of many critics has influenced the preparation of this edition. Therefore, I would like this acknowledgement to serve as a general tribute to all those who have acted as sources of inspiration.

Finally, I would like to thank Dr Victor Lee, the series editor, for his wit and encouragement which guided this book throughout, and Jan Doorly, the project manager, whose meticulous and prompt editing has been exemplary.

Elizabeth Gurr

Editors

Dr Victor Lee, the series editor, read English at University College, Cardiff. He was awarded a doctorate at Oxford University. He has taught at secondary and tertiary level, working at the Open University for 27 years. Victor Lee's experience as an examiner is very wide. He has been, for example, a Chief Examiner in English A-level for three different boards, stretching over a period of more than 30 years.

Elizabeth Gurr was born in New Zealand and educated there and at Oxford University. She has taught in schools, colleges and universities in England and Africa and was Head of English at a comprehensive school in Berkshire. She is married with three sons and the author of *Alexander Pope* in the Writer and Critics series (Oliver and Boyd).

Foreword

Oxford Student Texts are specifically aimed at presenting poetry and drama to an audience studying English literature at an advanced level. Each text is designed as an integrated whole consisting of four main parts. The first part sets the scene by discussing the context in which the work was written. The most important part of the book is the poetry or play itself, and it is suggested that the student reads this first without consulting the Notes or other secondary sources. To encourage students to follow this advice, the Notes are placed together after the text, not alongside it. Where help is needed, the Notes and Interpretations sections provide it.

The Notes perform two functions. First, they provide information and explain allusions. Second (this is where they differ from most texts at this level), they often raise questions of central concern to the interpretation of the poems or play being dealt with, particularly in the general note placed at the beginning of each set of notes.

The fourth part, the Interpretations section, deals with major issues of response to the particular selection of poetry or drama. One of the major aims of this part of the text is to emphasize that there is no one right answer to interpretation, but a series of approaches. Readers are given guidance as to what counts as evidence, but in the end left to make up their own minds as to which are the most suitable interpretations, or to add their own.

In these revised editions, the Interpretations section now addresses a wider range of issues. There is a more detailed treatment of context and critical history, for example. The section contains a number of activity-discussion sequences, although it must be stressed that these are optional. Significant issues about the poetry or play are raised, and readers are invited to tackle activities before proceeding to the discussion section, where possible responses to the questions raised are considered. Their main function is to engage readers actively in the ideas of the text.

At the end of each text there is also a list of Essay Questions. Whereas the activity-discussion sequences are aimed at increasing understanding of the literary work itself, these tasks are intended to help explore ideas about the poetry or play after the student has completed the reading of the work and the studying of the Notes and Interpretations. These tasks are particularly helpful for coursework projects or in preparing for an examination.

Victor Lee *Series Editor*

Around 1737–8 Francois Louis Roubiliac modelled a terra cotta bust of Pope from life. An anecdote records that Roubiliac observed that Pope's countenance 'was that of a person who had been much afflicted with headaches, and that he should have known the fact from the contracted appearance of the skin above the eyebrows'. The many portraits of Pope painted in his lifetime disguise, by various means, his physical defects; his short stature, hump-back and contorted facial features. The marble busts sculpted by Roubiliac from the terra cotta model shown above, probably come closest to Pope's true appearance.

Alexander Pope in Context

Alexander Pope was born in 1688, the year of the Glorious Revolution when James II fled to France in the face of civil riots against his Roman Catholicism and William and Mary were invited to become Protestant rulers of England. After the tumultuous years of the Civil War, fought partly on religious grounds, and the execution of Charles I; after the Puritan Commonwealth ruled by Cromwell and the re-instatement of the monarchy with the return of Charles II, what the majority of English people wanted was a king, but not a Catholic one. The Act of Settlement in 1701 ensured that future heirs to the throne must be Protestant.

Alexander Pope's parents were both Roman Catholic and Pope continued in this faith all his life, despite the legal restrictions and civil disadvantages which were imposed on Catholics after 1688. As a Roman Catholic, Pope could not attend University; he could not hold public office or practise a profession; he could not own property or live within ten miles of London. He was taxed double, besides suffering many petty restraints such as not being allowed to own fire-arms or a horse worth more than five pounds. In peaceful years some laws could be tacitly ignored but whenever the Government felt threatened, for example during the 1715 Jacobite rising, new laws were passed and lapsed laws were re-enforced. Catholics led financially insecure and civilly restricted lives. Yet Pope parried his friend Bishop Atterbury's plea to change his religion, 'that Accident to your Own Ease and Happiness', by claiming that he lacked ambition, suffered from poor health and that it would upset his mother. These excuses may have hidden a faith deeper than he cared to reveal to his Protestant friends.

Pope's father was a successful linen merchant in the City of London but in 1689 he gave up his business, possibly a cautious move in view of the restrictions imposed by William and Mary's Government. In 1692 he moved the family from the City to

Hammersmith, again probably a reaction to the ten-mile exclusion law, and in 1700 the family moved even further from London to a place which was bliss for the twelve-year-old boy, the village of Binfield in Windsor Forest. (The house was carefully bought by Pope's father in the names of his wife's Protestant nephews and 'in trust for his only son, Alexander Pope'.) Alexander Pope loved the Forest and made the first of his valuable friendships there with Sir William Trumbull, a former Secretary of State, and with a close-knit group of Berkshire Catholic gentry. Barred from civic life, under continual threat of financial penalties, many old Catholic families retreated to quiet, impoverished lives on their country estates. Although Alexander Pope later made his adult home as close to London as the law allowed, members of these Berkshire families remained his friends for life. It was for this close circle of Catholic friends that *The Rape of the Locke* was initially, and privately, written.

When Pope was about thirteen he caught a disease which seems to have been a form of spinal tuberculosis. It left him physically deformed. He never grew taller than four and a half feet. His body became twisted and hunchbacked and the effort of standing and moving showed in cords of tension which stood out in his face in later life. Inhibited by his appearance, although always ready to joke about it, ('the least thing like a man in England' he called himself) he never married. His enemies, and there were many later in his life, used his physical deformities to attack him: 'a crooked mind in a crooked body'; 'a little Monster'; 'indigested Lump'; 'distorted Elf'; 'hunchback'd Toad'; 'Ape'; 'grinning Monkey' are only a few of the things he was called. Pope claimed indifference, and gave as good as he got in his own writings but, revealingly, he kept records of these personal attacks, gathering them into four, bound volumes. They may have intensified his desire to acquire an ease in manners that he lacked in his physique.

During his teenage years at Binfield, as he recovered from the illness he had not expected to survive, Pope decided to become a poet. What did this mean? In the eighteenth century playwrights and pamphleteers could make a poor living as 'scribblers' but poetry was still seen as an accomplishment of leisured gentlemen, not a way of earning a livelihood. When he was seventeen Pope made his way back to London to show his manuscripts to the literary men to whom he was introduced in the fashionable coffee houses, the convenient meeting places of the day. In each of the next four years he spent several months in London, inviting criticism of his poems and re-working them. It was not until 1709 that he published his first poems, among them his translation of the episode of Sarpedon from the Iliad which he parodied in *The Rape*.

As a Catholic, Pope could not become Poet Laureate and, although offered, he refused all patronage. He secured independence with his translations of Homer's *Iliad* and *Odyssey*, each of which earned him between four and five thousand pounds. For *The Rape of the Lock* in 1714 he received only fifteen pounds. Although his poetry brought him financial security, it took a degree of planning which made Pope appear at times secretive, even conniving. He had to work hard to gain control of the publication of his work and to drum up the subscription lists which guaranteed sales.

In 1716, two months before the Act forbidding Catholics the right to own property became law, Pope's father sold the house at Binfield and the family moved to Chiswick under the protection of the Earl of Burlington. After his father's death a year later, Pope rented a house in Twickenham, close to his London friends and a safe enough distance to qualify under the ten-mile rule. Here, in semi-retirement with his mother, gardening and writing poetry, he lived modestly on the profits of his translations of Homer.

Fashioning a poet

Isolated and marginalized, Catholic and crippled, Pope was eager to be accepted in society at a time when, Woodman (See Further Reading) argues, manners were significant. The Court was becoming less relevant (especially under the 'foreign' Hanoverian rulers), social barriers were loosening and manners helped to define limits between the gentry and the vulgar. Politeness and refinement were social virtues which could be learned by an upwardly mobile merchant and professional class wishing to be accepted by the older, landed aristocracy. An important distinction became not the rank one was born into but how one behaved in society. In 1709 *The Tatler* was first published, followed in 1711 by *The Spectator*. These periodicals published gentle, humorous, essays making fun of the difference between uncouth and genteel behaviour.

In his writings, as in his behaviour, Pope aimed to appear well-bred, poised, and polished. He consciously fashioned a public image of himself as a gentleman and a poet and he had the highest ideals of what it meant to be a 'poet'. As Woodman wrote in 1997: 'Politeness is relevant not only to his self-presentation but also to his conception of the role of the poet'. Poetic writing must be polished, and Pope aimed at an ease which disguised the effort required to produce it. In his *Essay on Criticism* 1711 he writes:

> **True Ease in Writing comes from Art, not Chance,**
> **As those move easiest who have learn'd to dance.**

Pope assiduously re-worked his poems, especially in his earlier years, with what Dr Johnson called 'dilatory caution'. *The Rape* is an exception, having been written fast as an act of friendship, and the unusual speed of delivery may be one reason why he re-visited the poem, greatly enlarging it two years later.

Besides mastering technical excellence, Pope conceived of a 'poet' as a moral leader, someone who commented on the world rather than engaging with it, who, from the vantage point of self-chosen retirement from public life, was yet a leading spokesperson for the age. In his mature poems, the Horatian satires, Pope presents an ideal portrait of himself as honest, plain-living, retired, respected and above all, a satiric, moral force in his writings. Even *The Rape*, ostensibly a lightweight joke, had a serious purpose, to patch up a real quarrel, and its underlying theme is that manners matter and poetry has moral power.

The occasion of the poem

The occasion of the poem was a quarrel between two land-owning Roman Catholic families, the Petres and the Fermors. We know only the barest details of the incident from Pope himself, speaking to his friend Spence years later:

> The stealing of Miss Belle Fermor's hair was taken too seriously, and caused an estrangement between the two families, though they had lived long in great friendship before. A common acquaintance and well-wisher to both desired me to write a poem to make a jest of it, and laugh them together again.

Belle Fermor was a society beauty whose good looks had been celebrated in verse by several poets. Lord Petre was a young aristocrat who had succeeded to his estate in his teens under the guardianship of John Caryll. Pope barely knew Arabella. He never met Lord Petre. The Carylls were his Berkshire Catholic friends and it was John Caryll, the 'common acquaintance', who was the real instigator of the poem.

The youth of the principals suggests a romantic escapade, but if this was so the courtship was abortive. Before the poem was published Lord Petre was married, and not to Arabella who wed a Berkshire gentleman a few years later.

Versions

The Rape exists in three distinct versions. In answer to Caryll's request, Pope wrote his first two-canto poem quickly in 1711 and circulated it privately to the parties concerned (see Appendix 2, pp. 126–136). He published it 1712 in *Miscellaneous Poems and Translations*, a collection of poems by various poets. In 1714 Pope published the enlarged five-canto version, introducing *the Machinery* (the band of aerial beings) and adding a number of mock-epic incidents. Before the second version was published, Lord Petre had died of smallpox, Arabella had had second thoughts and Sir George Browne, caricatured as Sir Plume, was furious. Pope, somewhat annoyed at their reactions, may have wished to free *The Rape* from being a private piece. On the other hand, it was his usual practice to polish and re-work his writings. Whatever the reason, his additions place the poem more firmly in the mock-epic genre and his exchange of an intimate readership for a public one may account for the changes in his presentation of Belinda.

The 1714 version was an unusually prestigious and expensive publication – a single volume spreading the poem over 48 pages with six engraved pictures plus engraved head and tailpieces and initial letters. Within four days it sold over 3,000 copies. Pope gave Arabella the choice of two dedications, one prose, one poetry, the first naming her, the other protecting her anonymity. Arabella, apparently over her embarrassment, chose the prose dedication and later had her portrait painted wearing a sparkling cross and with a quotation from *The Rape* appended.

The third version was for Pope's collected *Works* 1717 when he added Clarissa's speech in Canto V, 'to open more clearly the MORAL of the poem', he explained. With some minor alterations taken from his 1726 edition of his *Works* this is the text which has been used for this edition.

The Rape of the Lock
an Heroi-comical Poem

Nolueram, Belinda, *tuos violare capillos;*
Sed juvat hoc precibus me tribuisse tuis.
MART.

To
Mrs Arabella Fermor

Madam,

It will be in vain to deny that I have some regard for this piece, since I dedicate it to You. Yet you may bear me witness, it was intended only to divert a few young Ladies, who have good sense and good humour enough to laugh not only at their sex's little unguarded follies, but at their own. But as it was communicated with the air of a Secret, it soon found its way into the world. An imperfect copy having been offer'd to a Bookseller, you had the good-nature for my sake to consent to the publication of one more correct: This I was forc'd to, before I had executed half my design, for the Machinery was entirely wanting to compleat it.

The Machinery, Madam, is a term invented by the Critics, to signify that part which the Deities, Angels, or Dæmons are made to act in a Poem: for the ancient Poets are in one respect like many modern Ladies; let an action be never so trivial in itself, they always make it appear of the utmost importance. These Machines I determin'd to raise on a very new and odd foundation, the *Rosicrucian* doctrine of Spirits.

I know how disagreeable it is to make use of hard words before a Lady; but 'tis so much the concern of a Poet to have his works understood, and particularly by your Sex, that you must give me leave to explain two or three difficult terms.

The *Rosicrucians* are a people I must bring you acquainted with. The best account I know of them is in a French book call'd *Le Comte de Gabalis*, which both in its title and size is so like a Novel, that many of the Fair Sex have read it for one by mistake. According to these Gentlemen, the four Elements are inhabited by Spirits, which they call *Sylphs*, *Gnomes*, *Nymphs*, and *Salamanders*. The *Gnomes* or Dæmons of Earth delight in mischief; but the *Sylphs*, whose habitation is in the Air, are the best-condition'd creatures imaginable. For they say, any mortals may enjoy the most intimate familiarities with these gentle Spirits, upon a condition very easy to all true Adepts, an inviolate preservation of Chastity.

As to the following Canto's, all the passages of them are as fabulous, as the Vision at the beginning, or the Transformation at the end; (except the loss of your Hair, which I always mention with reverence.) The Human persons are as fictitious as the Airy ones; and the character of *Belinda*, as it is now manag'd, resembles you in nothing but in Beauty.

If this Poem had as many Graces as there are in your Person, or in your Mind, yet I could never hope it should pass thro' the world half so Uncensur'd as You have done. But let its fortune be what it will, mine is happy enough, to have given me this occasion of assuring you that I am, with the truest esteem,

MADAM,
Your Most Obedient,
Humble Servant
A. POPE.

The Rape of the Lock

Canto I

What dire offence from am'rous causes springs,
What mighty contests rise from trivial things,
I sing – This verse to *Caryll*, Muse! is due:
This, ev'n *Belinda* may vouchsafe to view:
5 Slight is the subject, but not so the praise,
If She inspire, and He approve my lays.
    Say what strange motive, Goddess! could compel
A well-bred Lord t'assault a gentle *Belle*?
Oh say what stranger cause, yet unexplor'd,
10 Cou'd make a gentle *Belle* reject a Lord?
In tasks so bold, can little men engage,
And in soft bosoms dwells such mighty Rage?
    Sol thro' white curtains shot a tim'rous ray,
And ope'd those eyes that must eclipse the day;
15 Now lap-dogs give themselves the rousing shake,
And sleepless lovers, just at twelve, awake:
Thrice rung the bell, the slipper knock'd the ground,
And the press'd watch return'd a silver sound.
Belinda still her downy pillow prest,
20 Her guardian *Sylph* prolong'd the balmy rest:
'Twas he had summon'd to her silent bed
The morning-dream that hover'd o'er her head.
A Youth more glitt'ring than a Birth-night Beau,
(That ev'n in slumber caus'd her cheek to glow)
25 Seem'd to her ear his winning lips to lay,
And thus in whispers said, or seem'd to say.
    Fairest of mortals, thou distinguish'd care
Of thousand bright Inhabitants of Air!
If e'er one Vision touch'd thy infant thought,
30 Of all the Nurse and all the Priest have taught;

Of airy Elves by moonlight shadows seen,
The silver token, and the circled green,
Or virgins visited by Angel-pow'rs,
With golden crowns and wreaths of heav'nly flow'rs;
35 Hear and believe! thy own importance know,
Nor bound thy narrow views to things below.
Some secret truths, from learned pride conceal'd,
To Maids alone and Children are reveal'd:
What tho' no credit doubting Wits may give?
40 The Fair and Innocent shall still believe.
Know then, unnumber'd Spirits round thee fly,
The light Militia of the lower sky;
These, tho' unseen, are ever on the wing,
Hang o'er the Box, and hover round the Ring:
45 Think what an Equipage thou hast in Air,
And view with scorn two Pages and a Chair.
As now your own, our beings were of old,
And once inclos'd in Woman's beauteous mold;
Thence, by a soft transition, we repair
50 From earthly Vehicles to these of air.
Think not, when Woman's transient breath is fled,
That all her vanities at once are dead:
Succeeding vanities she still regards,
And tho' she plays no more, o'erlooks the cards.
55 Her joy in gilded Chariots, when alive,
And love of *Ombre*, after death survive.
For when the Fair in all the pride expire,
To their first Elements the Souls retire:
The Sprites of fiery Termagants in Flame
60 Mount up, and take a *Salamander's* name.
Soft yielding minds to Water glide away,
And sip, with *Nymphs*, their elemental Tea.
The graver Prude sinks downward to a *Gnome*,
In search of mischief still on Earth to roam.

65 The light Coquettes in *Sylphs* aloft repair,
And sport and flutter in the fields of Air.
　　Know farther yet; whoever fair and chaste
Rejects mankind, is by some *Sylph* embrac'd:
For Spirits, freed from mortal laws, with ease
70 Assume what sexes and what shapes they please.
What guards the purity of melting Maids
In courtly balls, and midnight masquerades,
Safe from the treach'rous friend, the daring spark,
The glance by day, the whisper in the dark,
75 When kind occasion prompts their warm desires,
When music softens, and when dancing fires?
'Tis but their *Sylph*, the wise Celestials know,
Tho' *Honour* is the word with Men below.
　　Some nymphs there are, too conscious of their face,
80 For life predestin'd to the *Gnomes* embrace.
These swell their prospects and exalt their pride,
When offers are disdain'd, and love deny'd:
Then gay Ideas crowd the vacant brain,
While Peers and Dukes, and all their sweeping train,
85 And Garters, Stars, and Coronets appear,
And in soft sounds, *Your Grace* salutes their ear.
'Tis these that early taint the female soul,
Instruct the eyes of young Coquettes to roll,
Teach Infant-cheeks a bidden blush to know,
90 And little hearts to flutter at a Beau.
　　Oft when the world imagine women stray,
The *Sylphs* thro' mystic mazes guide their way,
Thro' all the giddy circle they pursue,
And old impertinence expel by new.
95 What tender maid but must a victim fall
To one man's treat, but for another's ball?
When *Florio* speaks, what virgin could withstand,
If gentle *Damon* did not squeeze her hand?

With varying vanities, from ev'ry part,
100 They shift the moving Toyshop of their heart;
Where wigs with wigs, with sword-knots
    sword-knots strive,
Beaus banish beaus, and coaches coaches drive.
This erring mortals Levity may call,
Oh blind to truth! the *Sylphs* contrive it all.

105   Of these am I, who thy protection claim,
A watchful sprite, and *Ariel* is my name.
Late, as I rang'd the crystal wilds of air,
In the clear Mirror of thy ruling Star
I saw, alas! some dread event impend,
110 Ere to the main this morning sun descend.
But heav'n reveals not what, or how, or where:
Warn'd by the *Sylph*, oh pious maid, beware!
This to disclose is all thy guardian can.
Beware of all, but most beware of Man!

115   He said; when *Shock*, who thought she slept too long,
Leap'd up, and wak'd his mistress with his tongue.
'Twas then *Belinda*, if report say true,
Thy eyes first open'd on a Billet-doux;
Wounds, Charms, and Ardors, were no sooner read,
120 But all the Vision vanish'd from thy head.

    And now, unveil'd, the Toilet stands display'd,
Each silver Vase in mystic order laid.
First, rob'd in white, the nymph intent adores,
With head uncover'd, the Cosmetic pow'rs.
125 A heav'nly Image in the glass appears,
To that she bends, to that her eyes she rears;
Th'inferior Priestess, at her altar's side,
Trembling, begins the sacred rites of Pride.
Unnumber'd treasures ope at once, and here
130 The various off'rings of the world appear;
From each she nicely culls with curious toil,

And decks the Goddess with the glitt'ring spoil.
This casket *India's* glowing gems unlocks,
And all *Arabia* breathes from yonder box.
135 The Tortoise here and Elephant unite,
Tranform'd to combs, the speckled, and the white.
Here files of pins extend their shining rows,
Puffs, Powders, Patches, Bibles, Billet-doux.
Now awful Beauty puts on all its arms;
140 The fair each moment rises in her charms,
Repairs her smiles, awakens ev'ry grace,
And calls forth all the wonders of her face;
Sees by degrees a purer blush arise,
And keener lightnings quicken in her eyes.
145 The busy *Sylphs* surround their darling care,
These set the head, and those divide the hair,
Some fold the sleeve, while others plait the gown;
And *Betty's* prais'd for labours not her own.

Canto II

Not with more glories, in th'etherial plain,
The Sun first rises o'er the purpled main,
Than issuing forth, the rival of his beams
Lanch'd on the bosom of the silver *Thames*.
5 Fair Nymphs, and well-drest Youths around her shone,
But ev'ry eye was fix'd on her alone.
On her white breast a sparkling Cross she wore,
Which Jews might kiss, and Infidels adore.
Her lively looks a sprightly mind disclose,
10 Quick as her eyes, and as unfix'd as those:
Favours to none, to all she smiles extends,
Oft she rejects, but never once offends.
Bright as the sun, her eyes the gazers strike,

And, like the sun, they shine on all alike.
15 Yet graceful ease, and sweetness void of pride
Might hide her faults, if *Belles* had faults to hide:
If to her share some female errors fall,
Look on her face, and you'll forget 'em all.
    This Nymph, to the destruction of mankind,
20 Nourish'd two Locks, which graceful hung behind
In equal curls, and well conspir'd to deck
With shining ringlets the smooth iv'ry neck:
Love in these labyrinths his slaves detains,
And mighty hearts are held in slender chains.
25 With hairy sprindges we the birds betray,
Slight lines of hair surprize the finny prey,
Fair tresses man's imperial race insnare,
And beauty draws us with a single hair.
    Th' advent'rous Baron the bright locks admir'd,
30 He saw, he wish'd, and to the prize aspir'd.
Resolv'd to win, he meditates the way,
By force to ravish, or by fraud betray;
For when success a Lover's toil attends,
Few ask, if fraud or force attain'd his ends.
35   For this, ere *Phœbus* rose, he had implor'd
Propitious heav'n, and ev'ry pow'r ador'd,
But chiefly Love – to Love an altar built,
Of twelve vast *French* Romances, neatly gilt.
There lay three garters, half a pair of gloves;
40 And all the trophies of his former loves.
With tender Billet-doux he lights the pyre,
And breathes three am'rous sighs to raise the fire.
Then prostrate falls, and begs with ardent eyes
Soon to obtain, and long possess the prize:
45 The Pow'rs gave ear, and granted half his pray'r,
The rest, the winds dispers'd in empty air.
    But now secure the painted vessel glides,

The sun-beams trembling on the floating tydes;
While melting music steals upon the sky,
50 And soften'd sounds along the waters die;
Smooth flow the waves, the Zephyrs gently play,
Belinda smil'd, and all the world was gay.
All but the *Sylph* – with careful thoughts opprest,
Th'impending woe sate heavy on his breast.
55 He summons strait his Denizens of air;
The lucid squadrons round the sails repair:
Soft o'er the shrouds aërial whispers breathe,
That seem'd but Zephyrs to the train beneath.
Some to the sun their insect-wings unfold,
60 Waft on the breeze, or sink in clouds of gold;
Transparent forms, too fine for mortal sight,
Their fluid bodies half dissolv'd in light.
Loose to the wind their airy garments flew,
Thin glitt'ring textures of the filmy dew,
65 Dipt in the richest tincture of the skies,
Where light disports in ever-mingling dyes,
While ev'ry beam new transient colours flings,
Colours that change whene'er they wave their wings.
Amid the circle, on the gilded mast,
70 Superior by the head, was *Ariel* plac'd;
His purple pinions opening to the sun,
He rais'd his azure wand, and thus begun.
  Ye *Sylphs* and *Sylphids*, to your chief give ear,
Fays, Fairies, Genii, Elves, and *Dæmons* hear!
75 Ye know the spheres and various tasks assign'd
By laws eternal to th'aërial kind.
Some in the fields of purest *Æther* play,
And bask and whiten in the blaze of day.
Some guide the course of wand'ring orbs on high,
80 Or roll the planets thro' the boundless sky.
Some less refin'd, beneath the moon's pale light

Pursue the stars that shoot athwart the night,
Or suck the mists in grosser air below,
Or dip their pinions in the painted bow,
85 Or brew fierce tempests on the wintry main,
Or o'er the glebe distil the kindly rain.
Others on earth o'er human race preside,
Watch all their ways, and all their actions guide:
Of these the chief the care of Nations own,
90 And guard with Arms divide the *British* Throne.
   Our humbler province is to tend the Fair;
Not a less pleasing, tho' less glorious care:
To save the powder from too rude a gale,
Nor let th'imprison'd essences exhale;
95 To draw fresh colours from the vernal flow'rs;
To steal from rainbows ere they drop in show'rs
A brighter wash; to curl their waving hairs,
Assist their blushes, and inspire their airs;
Nay oft, in dreams, invention we bestow,
100 To change a Flounce, or add a Furbelow.
   This day, black Omens threat the brightest Fair
That e'er deserv'd a watchful spirit's care;
Some dire disaster, or by force or slight;
But what, or where, the fates have wrapt in night.
105 Whether the nymph shall break *Diana's* law,
Or some frail *China* jar receive a flaw,
Or stain her honour, or her new brocade,
Forget her pray'rs, or miss a masquerade,
Or lose her heart, or necklace, at a ball;
110 Or whether Heav'n has doom'd that *Shock* must fall.
Haste then, ye spirits! to your charge repair;
The flutt'ring fan be *Zephyretta's* care;
The drops to thee, *Brillante*, we consign;
And, *Momentilla*, let the watch be thine;
115 Do thou, *Crispissa*, tend her fav'rite Lock;

    Ariel himself shall be the guard of *Shock*.
      To fifty chosen *Sylphs*, of special note,
    We trust th' important charge, the Petticoat:
    Oft have we known that seven-fold fence to fail,
120 Tho' stiff with hoops, and arm'd with ribs of whale.
    Form a strong line about the silver bound,
    And guard the wide circumference around.
      Whatever spirit, careless of his charge,
    His post neglects, or leaves the fair at large,
125 Shall feel sharp vengeance soon o'ertake his sins,
    Be stop'd in vials, or transfix'd with pins;
    Or plung'd in lakes of bitter washes lie,
    Or wedg'd whole ages in a bodkin's eye:
    Gums and Pomatums shall his flight restrain,
130 While clog'd he beats his silken wings in vain;
    Or Alom stypticks with contracting pow'r
    Shrink his thin essence like a rivell'd flow'r:
    Or as *Ixion* fix'd, the wretch shall feel
    The giddy motion of the whirling Mill,
135 In fumes of burning Chocolate shall glow,
    And tremble at the sea that froaths below!
      He spoke; the spirits from the sails descend;
    Some, orb in orb, around the nymph extend;
    Some thrid the mazy ringlets of her hair;
140 Some hang upon the pendants of her ear;
    With beating hearts the dire event they wait,
    Anxious, and trembling for the birth of Fate.

Canto III

    Close by those meads, for ever crown'd with flow'rs,
    Where *Thames* with pride surveys his rising tow'rs,
    There stands a structure of majestic frame,

Which from the neighb'ring *Hampton* takes it name.
5 Here *Britain's* statesmen oft the fall foredoom
Of foreign Tyrants, and of Nymphs at home;
Here thou, great ANNA! whom three realms obey,
Dost sometimes counsel take – and sometimes Tea.
   Hither the heroes and the nymphs resort,
10 To taste a while the pleasures of a Court;
In various talk th'instructive hours they past,
Who gave the ball, or paid the visit last;
One speaks the glory of the *British* Queen,
And one describes a charming *Indian* screen;
15 A third interprets motions, looks, and eyes;
At ev'ry word a reputation dies.
Snuff, or the fan, supply each pause of chat,
With singing, laughing, ogling, and all that.
   Mean while declining from the noon of day,
20 The sun obliquely shoots his burning ray;
The hungry Judges soon the sentence sign,
And wretches hang that jury-men may dine;
The merchant from th'*Exchange* returns in peace,
And the long labours of the Toilet cease.
25 *Belinda* now, whom thirst of fame invites,
Burns to encounter two advent'rous Knights,
At *Ombre* singly to decide their doom;
And swells her breast with conquests yet to come.
Strait the three bands prepare in arms to join,
30 Each band the number of the sacred nine.
Soon as she spreads her hand, th'aërial guard
Descend, and sit on each important card:
First *Ariel* perch'd upon a Matadore,
Then each, according to the rank they bore;
35 For *Sylphs*, yet mindful of their ancient race,
Are, as when women, wondrous fond of place.
   Behold, four Kings in majesty rever'd,

With hoary whiskers and a forky beard;
And four fair Queens whose hands sustain a flow'r,
40 Th'expressive emblem of their softer pow'r;
Four Knaves in garbs succinct, a trusty band,
Caps on their heads, and halberts in their hand;
And particolour'd troops, a shining train,
Draw forth to combat on the velvet plain.
45   The skilful Nymph reviews her force with care:
Let Spades be trumps! she said, and trumps they were.
   Now move to war her sable Matadores,
In show like leaders of the swarthy Moors.
Spadillio first, unconquerable Lord!
50 Led off two captive trumps, and swept the board.
As many more *Manillio* forc'd to yield,
And march'd a victor from the verdant field.
Him *Basto* follow'd, but his fate more hard
Gain'd but one trump and one *Plebeian* card.
55 With his broad sabre next, a chief in years,
The hoary Majesty of Spades appears,
Puts forth one manly leg, to sight reveal'd,
The rest, his many-coloured robe conceal'd.
The rebel Knave, who dares his prince engage,
60 Proves the just victim of his royal rage.
Ev'n mighty *Pam*, that Kings and Queens o'erthrew
And mow'd down armies in the fights of *Lu*,
Sad chance of war! now destitute of aid,
Falls undistinguish'd by the victor Spade!
65   Thus far both armies to *Belinda* yield;
Now to the Baron fate inclines the field.
His warlike *Amazon* her host invades,
Th'imperial consort of the crown of Spades.
The Club's black Tyrant first her victim dy'd,
70 Spite of his haughty mien, and barb'rous pride:
What boots the regal circle on his head,

His giant limbs, in state unwieldy spread;
That long behind he trails his pompous robe,
And, of all monarchs, only grasps the globe?
75   The Baron now his Diamonds pours apace;
Th'embroider'd King who shows but half his face,
And his refulgent Queen, with powr's combin'd,
Of broken troops an easy conquest find.
Clubs, Diamonds, Hearts, in wild disorder seen,
80 With throngs promiscuous strow the level green.
Thus when dispers'd a routed army runs,
Of *Asia's* troops, and *Afric's* sable sons,
With like confusion different nations fly,
Of various habit, and of various dye,
85 The pierc'd batallions dis-united fall,
In heaps on heaps; one fate o'erwhelms them all.
       The Knave of Diamonds tries his wily arts,
And wins (oh shameful chance!) the Queen of Hearts.
At this, the blood the virgin's cheek forsook,
90 A livid paleness spreads o'er all her look;
She sees, and trembles at th' approaching ill,
Just in the jaws of ruin, and *Codille*.
And now, (as oft in some distemper'd State)
On one nice Trick depends the gen'ral fate.
95 An Ace of Hearts steps forth: The King unseen
Lurk'd in her hand, and mourn'd his captive Queen:
He springs to vengeance with an eager pace,
And falls like thunder on the prostrate Ace.
The nymph exulting fills with shouts the sky;
100 The walls, the woods, and long canals reply.
       Oh thoughtless mortals! ever blind to fate,
Too soon dejected, and too soon elate!
Sudden, these honours shall be snatch'd away,
And curs'd for ever this victorious day.
105   For lo! the board with cups and spoons is crown'd,

The berries crackle, and the mill turns round;
On shining Altars of *Japan* they raise
The silver lamp; the fiery spirits blaze:
From silver spouts the grateful liquors glide,
110 While *China's* earth receives the smoaking tyde:
At once they gratify their scent and taste,
And frequent cups prolong the rich repaste.
Strait hover round the Fair her airy band;
Some, as she sipp'd, the fuming liquor fann'd,
115 Some o'er her lap their careful plumes display'd,
Trembling, and conscious of the rich brocade.
Coffee, (which makes the politician wise,
And see thro' all things with his half-shut eyes)
Sent up in vapours to the Baron's brain
120 New stratagems, the radiant Lock to gain.
Ah cease, rash youth! desist ere 'tis too late,
Fear the just Gods, and think of Scylla's Fate!
Chang'd to a bird, and sent to flit in air,
She dearly pays for *Nisus'* injur'd hair!
125   But when to mischief mortals bend their will,
How soon they find fit instruments of ill?
Just then, *Clarissa* drew with tempting grace
A two-edg'd weapon from her shining case;
So Ladies in Romance assist their Knight,
130 Present the spear, and arm him for the fight.
He takes the gift with rev'rence, and extends
The little engine on his finger's ends;
This just behind *Belinda's* neck he spread,
As o'er the fragrant steams she bends her head.
135 Swift to the Lock a thousand Sprites repair,
A thousand wings, by turns, blow back the hair;
And thrice they twitch'd the diamond in her ear;
Thrice she look'd back, and thrice the foe drew near.
Just in that instance, anxious *Ariel* sought

140 The close recesses of the Virgin's thought;
  As on the nosegay in her breast reclin'd,
  He watch'd th' Ideas rising in her mind,
  Sudden he view'd, in spite of all her art,
  An earthly Lover lurking at her heart.
145 Amaz'd, confus'd, he found his pow'r expir'd,
  Resign'd to fate, and with a sigh retir'd.
    The Peer now spreads the glitt'ring *Forfex* wide,
  T'inclose the Lock; now joins it, to divide.
  Ev'n then, before the fatal engine clos'd,
150 A wretched *Sylph* too fondly interpos'd;
  Fate urg'd the sheers, and cut the *Sylph* in twain,
  (But airy substance soon unites again)
  The meeting points the sacred hair dissever
  From the fair head, for ever, and for ever!
155   Then flash'd the living lightning from her eyes,
  And screams of horror rend th'affrighted skies.
  Not louder shrieks to pitying heav'n are cast,
  When husbands or when lapdogs breathe their last;
  Or when rich *China* vessels fall'n from high,
160 In glitt'ring dust, and painted fragments lie!
    Let wreaths of triumph now my temples twine,
  (The Victor cry'd) the glorious Prize is mine!
  While fish in streams, or birds delight in air,
  Or in a Coach and six the *British* Fair,
165 As long as *Atalantis* shall be read,
  Or the small pillow grace a Lady's bed,
  While visits shall be paid on solemn days,
  When num'rous wax-lights in bright order blaze,
  While nymphs take treats, or assignations give,
170 So long my honour, name, and praise shall live!
    What Time wou'd spare, from Steel receives its date,
  And monuments, like men, submit to fate!
  Steel could the labour of the Gods destroy,

And strike to dust th'imperial tow'rs of *Troy*;
175 Steel could the works of mortal pride confound,
And hew triumphal arches to the ground.
What wonder then, fair nymph! thy hairs shou'd feel
The conqu'ring force of unresisted steel?

Canto IV

But anxious cares the pensive nymph oppress'd,
And secret passions labour'd in her breast.
Not youthful kings in battle seiz'd alive,
Not scornful virgins who their charms survive,
5 Not ardent lovers robb'd of all their bliss,
Not ancient ladies when refus'd a kiss,
Not tyrants fierce that unrepenting die,
Not *Cynthia* when her manteau's pinn'd awry,
E'er felt such rage, resentment, and despair,
10 As thou, sad Virgin! for thy ravish'd Hair.
    For, that sad moment, when the *Sylphs* withdrew,
And *Ariel* weeping from *Belinda* flew,
Umbriel, a dusky, melancholy sprite,
As ever sully'd the fair face of light,
15 Down to the central earth, his proper scene,
Repair'd to search the gloomy Cave of *Spleen*.
    Swift on his sooty pinions flits the *Gnome*,
And in a vapour reach'd the dismal dome.
No chearful breeze this sullen region knows,
20 The dreaded East is all the wind that blows.
Here in a grotto, shelter'd close from air,
And screen'd in shades from day's detested glare,
She sighs for ever on her pensive bed,
Pain at her side, and *Megrim* at her head.
25   Two handmaids wait the throne: alike in place,

But diff'ring far in figure and in face.
Here stood *Ill-nature* like an ancient maid,
Her wrinkled form in black and white array'd;
With store of pray'rs, for mornings, nights, and noons,
30 Her hand is fill'd; her bosom with lampoons.
　　There *Affectation*, with a sickly mien,
Shows in her cheek the roses of eighteen,
Practis'd to lisp, and hang the head aside,
Faints into airs, and languishes with pride,
35 On the rich quilt sinks with becoming woe,
Wrapt in a gown, for sickness and for show.
The fair-ones feel such maladies as these,
When each new night-dress gives a new disease.
　　A constant Vapour o'er the palace flies;
40 Strange phantoms rising as the mists arise;
Dreadful, as hermit's dreams in haunted shades,
Or bright, as visions of expiring maids.
Now glaring fiends, and snakes on rolling spires,
Pale spectres, gaping tombs, and purple fires:
45 Now lakes of liquid gold, *Elysian* scenes,
And crystal domes, and Angels in machines.
　　Unnumber'd throngs on ev'ry side are seen,
Of bodies chang'd to various forms by Spleen.
Here living Tea-pots stand, one arm held out,
50 One bent; the handle this, and that the spout:
A Pipkin there, like *Homer's* Tripod walks;
Here sighs a Jar, and there a Goose-pye talks;
Men prove with child, as pow'rful fancy works,
And maids turn'd bottles, call aloud for corks.
55 　　Safe past the *Gnome* thro' this fantastic band,
A branch of healing Spleenwort in his hand.
Then thus address'd the pow'r – Hail wayward Queen!
Who rule the sex to fifty from fifteen:
Parent of vapours and of female wit,

60 Who give th' hysteric, or poetic fit,
On various tempers act by various ways,
Make some take physic, others scribble plays;
Who cause the proud their visits to delay,
And send the godly in a pett, to pray.
65 A Nymph there is, that all thy pow'r disdains,
And thousands more in equal mirth maintains.
But oh! if e'er thy *Gnome* could spoil a grace,
Or raise a pimple on a beauteous face,
Like Citron-waters matrons cheeks inflame,
70 Or change complexions at a losing game;
If e'er with airy horns I planted heads,
Or rumpled petticoats, or tumbled beds,
Or caus'd suspicion when no soul was rude,
Or discompos'd the head-dress of a Prude,
75 Or e'er to costive lap-dog gave disease,
Which not the tears of brightest eyes could ease:
Hear me, and touch *Belinda* with chagrin:
That single act gives half the world the spleen.
The Goddess with a discontented air
80 Seems to reject him, tho' she grants his pray'r.
A wond'rous Bag with both her hands she binds,
Like that where once *Ulysses* held the winds;
There she collects the force of female lungs,
Sighs, sobs, and passions, and the war of tongues.
85 A Vial next she fills with fainting fears,
Soft sorrows, melting griefs, and flowing tears.
The *Gnome* rejoicing bears her gifts away,
Spreads his black wings, and slowly mounts to day.
Sunk in *Thalestris'* arms the nymph he found,
90 Her eyes dejected and her hair unbound.
Full o'er their heads the swelling bag he rent,
And all the Furies issued at the vent.
Belinda burns with more than mortal ire,

And fierce *Thalestris* fans the rising fire.
95 O wretched maid! she spread her hands, and cry'd,
(While *Hampton's* echoes, wretched maid! reply'd)
Was it for this you took such constant care
The bodkin, comb, and essence to prepare?
For this your locks in paper durance bound,
100 For this with tort'ring irons wreath'd around?
For this with fillets strain'd your tender head,
And bravely bore the double loads of lead?
Gods! shall the ravisher display your hair,
While the Fops envy, and the Ladies stare!
105 *Honour* forbid! at whose unrival'd shrine
Ease, pleasure, virtue, all, our sex resign.
Methinks already I your tears survey,
Already hear the horrid things they say,
Already see you a degraded toast,
110 And all your honour in a whisper lost!
How shall I, then, your helpless fame defend?
'Twill then be infamy to seem your friend!
And shall this prize, th' inestimable prize,
Expos'd thro' crystal to the gazing eyes,
115 And heightened by the diamond's circling rays,
On that rapacious hand for ever blaze?
Sooner shall grass in *Hyde-Park Circus* grow,
And wits take lodgings in the sound of *Bow*;
Sooner let earth, air, sea, to *Chaos* fall,
120 Men, monkeys, lap-dogs, parrots, perish all!
    She said; then raging to Sir *Plume* repairs,
And bids her Beau demand the precious hairs:
(Sir *Plume*, of amber Snuff-box justly vain,
And the nice conduct of a clouded cane)
125 With earnest eyes, and round unthinking face,
He first the snuff-box open'd, then the case,
And thus broke out – 'My Lord, why, what the devil?

'Z——ds! damn the lock! 'fore Gad, you must be civil!
'Plague on't! 'tis past a jest – nay prithee, pox!
130 'Give her the hair' – he spoke, and rapp'd his box.
  It grieves me much (reply'd the Peer again)
Who speaks so well should ever speak in vain.
But by this Lock, this sacred Lock I swear,
(Which never more shall join its parted hair;
135 Which never more its honours shall renew,
Clip'd from the lovely head where late it grew)
That while my nostrils draw the vital air,
This hand which won it, shall for ever wear.
He spoke, and speaking, in proud triumph spread
140 The long-contended honours of her head.
  But *Umbriel*, hateful *Gnome*! forbears not so;
He breaks the Vial whence the sorrows flow.
Then see! the nymph in beauteous grief appears,
Her eyes half-languishing, half-drown'd in tears;
145 On her heav'd bosom hung her drooping head,
Which, with a sigh, she rais'd; and thus she said.
  For ever curs'd be this detested day,
Which snatch'd my best, my fav'rite curl away!
Happy! ah ten times happy had I been,
150 If *Hampton-Court* these eyes had never seen!
Yet am not I the first mistaken maid,
By love of Courts to num'rous ills betray'd.
Oh had I rather un-admir'd remain'd
In some lone isle, or distant Northern land;
155 Where the gilt Chariot never marks the way,
Where none learn *Ombre*, none e'er taste *Bohea*!
There kept my charms conceal'd from mortal eye,
Like roses, that in desarts bloom and die.
What mov'd my mind with youthful Lords to roam?
160 O had I stay'd, and said my pray'rs at home!
'Twas this, the morning omens seem'd to tell;

Thrice from my trembling hand the patch-box fell;
The tott'ring China shook without a wind,
Nay *Poll* sat mute, and *Shock* was most unkind!
165 A *Sylph* too warn'd me of the threats of fate,
In mystic visions, now believ'd too late!
See the poor remnants of these slighted hairs!
My hands shall rend what ev'n thy rapine spares:
These, in two sable ringlets taught to break,
170 Once gave new beauties to the snowy neck;
The sister-lock now sits uncouth, alone,
And in its fellow's fate foresees its own;
Uncurl'd it hangs, the fatal sheers demands,
And tempts once more thy sacrilegious hands.
175 Oh hadst thou, cruel! been content to seize
Hairs less in sight, or any hairs but these!

Canto V

She said: the pitying audience melt in tears.
But Fate and *Jove* had stopp'd the Baron's ears.
In vain *Thalestris* with reproach assails,
For who can move when fair *Belinda* fails?
5 Not half so fix'd the *Trojan* could remain,
While *Anna* begg'd and *Dido* rag'd in vain.
Then grave *Clarissa* graceful wav'd her fan;
Silence ensu'd, and thus the nymph began.
  Say why are Beauties prais'd and honour'd most,
10 The wise man's passion, and the vain man's toast?
Why deck'd with all that land and sea afford,
Why Angels call'd, and Angel-like ador'd?
Why round our coaches crowd the white-glov'd Beaus,
Why bows the side-box from its inmost rows?
15 How vain are all these glories, all our pains,

Unless good sense preserve what beauty gains:
That men may say when we the front-box grace,
Behold the first in virtue, as in face!
Oh! if to dance all night, and dress all day,
20 Charm'd the small-pox, or chas'd old-age away;
Who would not scorn what housewife's cares produce,
Or who would learn one earthly thing of use?
To patch, nay ogle, might become a Saint,
Nor could it sure be such a sin to paint.
25 But since, alas! frail beauty must decay,
Curl'd or uncurl'd, since Locks will turn to grey;
Since painted, or not painted, all shall fade,
And she who scorns a man, must die a maid;
What then remains but well our pow'r to use,
30 And keep good-humour still whate'er we lose?
And trust me, dear! good-humour can prevail,
When airs, and flights, and screams, and scolding fail.
Beauties in vain their pretty eyes may roll;
Charms strike the sight, but merit wins the soul.
35   So spoke the Dame, but no applause ensu'd;
Belinda frown'd, *Thalestris* call'd her Prude.
To arms, to arms! the fierce Virago cries,
And swift as lightning to the combat flies.
All side in parties, and begin th' attack;
40 Fans clap, silks russle and tough whalebones crack;
Heroes and Heroines shouts confus'dly rise,
And base, and treble voices strike the skies.
No common weapons in their hands are found,
Like Gods they fight, nor dread a mortal wound.
45   So when bold *Homer* makes the Gods engage,
And heav'nly breasts with human passions rage;
'Gainst *Pallas, Mars; Latona, Hermes* arms;
And all *Olympus* rings with loud alarms:
Jove's thunder roars, heav'n trembles all around;

50　Blue *Neptune* storms, the bellowing deeps resound;
　　Earth shakes her nodding tow'rs, the ground gives wa
　　And the pale ghosts start at the flash of day!
　　　Triumphant *Umbriel* on a sconce's height
　　Clap'd his glad wings, and sate to view the fight:
55　Prop'd on their bodkin spears, the Sprites survey
　　The growing combat, or assist the fray.
　　　While thro' the press enrag'd *Thalestris* flies,
　　And scatters deaths around from both her eyes,
　　A Beau and Witling perish'd in the throng,
60　One dy'd in metaphor, and one in song.
　　'O cruel nymph! a living death I bear'
　　Cry'd *Dapperwit*, and sunk beside his chair.
　　A mournful glance Sir *Fopling* upwards cast,
　　Those eyes are made so killing – was his last.
65　Thus on *Mæander*'s flow'ry margin lies
　　Th' expiring *Swan*, and as he sings he dies.
　　　When bold Sir *Plume* had drawn *Clarissa* down,
　　Chloe stepp'd in, and kill'd him with a frown;
　　She smil'd to see the doughty hero slain,
70　But, at her smile, the Beau reviv'd again.
　　　Now *Jove* suspends his golden scales in air,
　　Weighs the Men's wits against the Lady's hair;
　　The doubtful beam long nods from side to side;
　　At length the wits mount up, the hairs subside.
75　　See fierce *Belinda* on the Baron flies,
　　With more than usual lightning in her eyes:
　　Nor fear'd the Chief th'unequal fight to try,
　　Who sought no more than on his foe to die.
　　But this bold Lord with manly strength endu'd,
80　She with one finger and a thumb subdu'd:
　　Just where the breath of life his nostrils drew,
　　A charge of Snuff the wily virgin threw;
　　The *Gnomes* direct, to ev'ry atome just,

The pungent grains of titillating dust.
85 Sudden, with starting tears each eye o'erflows,
And the high dome re-echoes to his nose.
Now meet thy fate, incens'd *Belinda* cry'd,
And drew a deadly bodkin from her side.
(The same, his ancient personage to deck,
90 Her great great grandsire wore about his neck,
In three seal-rings; which after, melted down,
Form'd a vast buckle for his widow's gown:
Her infant grandame's whistle next it grew,
The bells she jingled, and the whistle blew;
95 Then in a bodkin grac'd her mother's hairs,
Which long she wore, and now *Belinda* wears.)
Boast not my fall (he cry'd) insulting foe!
Thou by some other shalt be laid as low.
Nor think, to die dejects my lofty mind:
100 All that I dread is leaving you behind!
Rather than so, ah let me still survive,
And burn in *Cupid's* flames, – but burn alive.
Restore the Lock! she cries; and all around
Restore the Lock! the vaulted roofs rebound.
105 Not fierce *Othello* in so loud a strain
Roar'd for the handkerchief that caus'd his pain.
But see how oft ambitious aims are cross'd,
And chiefs contend 'till all the prize is lost!
The Lock, obtain'd with guilt, and kept with pain,
110 In ev'ry place is sought, but sought in vain:
With such a prize no mortal must be blest,
So heav'n decrees! with heav'n who can contest?
Some thought it mounted to the Lunar sphere,
Since all things lost on earth are treasur'd there.
115 There Hero's wits are kept in pond'rous vases,
And Beau's in snuff-boxes and tweezer-cases.
There broken vows, and death-bed alms are found,

And lover's hearts with ends of ribband bound,
The courtier's promises, and sick man's pray'rs,
120 The smiles of harlots, and the tears of heirs,
Cages for gnats, and chains to yoak a flea,
Dry'd butterflies, and tomes of casuistry.
    But trust the Muse – she saw it upward rise,
Tho' mark'd by none but quick, poetic eyes:
125 (So *Rome's* great founder to the heav'ns withdrew,
To *Proculus* alone confess'd in view)
A sudden Star, it shot thro' liquid air,
And drew behind a radiant trail of hair.
Not *Berenice's* Locks first rose so bright,
130 The heav'ns bespangling with dishevel'd light,
The *Sylphs* behold it kindling as it flies,
And pleas'd pursue its progress thro' the skies.
    This the *Beau-monde* shall from the Mall survey,
And hail with music its propitious ray.
135 This the blest Lover shall for *Venus* take,
And send up vows from *Rosamonda's* lake.
This *Partridge* soon shall view in cloudless skies,
When next he looks thro' *Galilæo's* eyes;
And hence th'egregious wizard shall foredoom
140 The fate of *Louis*, and the fall of *Rome*.
    Then cease, bright Nymph! to mourn thy ravish'd hair
Which adds new glory to the shining sphere!
Not all the tresses that fair head can boast,
Shall draw such envy as the Lock you lost.
145 For, after all the murders of your eye,
When, after millions slain, yourself shall die;
When those fair suns shall set, as set they must,
And all those tresses shall be laid in dust;
This Lock, the Muse shall consecrate to fame,
150 And 'midst the stars inscribe *Belinda's* name.

Notes

Canto I: Lines 1–12

Pope imitates the customary style of an epic by first proposing his subject and then praying for inspiration. But by line 3 he has already turned the convention on its head. (See p. 73–4 in Interpretations.) In these opening lines the mock-heroic tone is exhibited, but is it clear what is being mocked? What is the effect of elevating the quarrel between the Fermors and Petres into *mighty contests* while calling the loss of a curl a *trivial thing*? Is Pope using the mock-heroic style to make a jest of the occasion of the poem or does the high style of the epic opening, with its inverted syntax and declamatory tone, lend dignity to a subject which Pope calls *Slight*?

3 **Caryll, Muse** John Caryll, a Roman Catholic and dear friend to Pope, knew both families concerned in the incident. He had been guardian to Lord Petre. The *Muse* was the goddess of poetry, one of the nine sister-goddesses who inspired the sciences and the arts. Although Pope's dedication to a human carries the joking implication that his subject may be insufficiently grand to require heavenly assistance, in all sincerity much was due to Caryll.

4 **ev'n Belinda** is the tone one of flattery or mockery? The word *ev'n* could be Pope laughing at Belinda's lack of interest in reading poetry (unless addressed to her personally) or he could be paying her a compliment which, although extravagant, is genuine.

6 **lays** poems. The word originally referred to poems which were sung. It was believed in the eighteenth century that Homer and Virgil had sung their epics. Pope echoes Virgil's famous opening line in the *Aeneid*, *Arms and the Man I sing*, by claiming that he too is singing this poem.

7–8 Pope's wide-eyed claim that he cannot understand what attracts a man to a woman is a knowing joke he expects the reader to share. The word *compel* raised questions from the start. John

33

Dennis, one of Pope's severest critics, objected at the time that it *supposes the Baron to be a Beast, not a free agent*. What difference would it make if Pope had written 'induce' or 'provoke'? The hint of compulsion may be a tribute to the power of female beauty; equally it may be trying to excuse the male advance. The same question of who is being blamed arises with the word *assault*. To what extent are the military and sexual connotations of the word brought into play? Pope may be using the word to point the narrative forward to the battle that forms the climax of the plot or it could be a sexual metaphor. The feeling of the word is aggressive, implying danger. How far is this softened by the phrase *well-bred*, suggesting that what has happened is merely a breach of polite behaviour?

8 **Belle** a pretty young woman. Belles and beaux (handsomely dressed young men) were terms commonly used in the late seventeenth and eighteenth centuries to refer to the fashionable young set.

9 **unexplor'd** undiscovered.

9–12 Is the irony at the expense of men or women or both? *Little men* is a mock-heroic joke, ironically contrasting contemporary male endeavours with what an epic hero would perform in *tasks so bold*. The tone of the phrase *stranger cause* raises questions. Is it teasing and affectionate or is there a sharper note, implying that any girl would be delighted to catch a lord and unlikely to refuse his advances?

Lines 13–120

The action of the poem runs through the space of a single day, a day defined by the heroine. It starts late with Belinda's noon awakening and ends at night under the light of a newly created star. Belinda's guardian sylph, Ariel (not named until I 106), instructs her in a dream about the unseen *bright Inhabitants of Air* (28), who accompany and protect women. In his introductory letter to Arabella Fermor in the 1714 edition, Pope claimed that he took the idea for these elemental sprites from a light-weight romantic book,

Le Comte de Gabalis, based on the philosophical theories of the Rosicrucians, a minor seventeenth-century semi-religious, semi-philosophical society. He added freely from fairy tale and superstition (*all the Nurse and all the Priest have taught* [30]).

The sylphs are Pope's substitute for the gods in an epic who control the fortunes of the hero and direct the outcome of events. As he did not introduce them until he expanded *The Rape* in 1714, and as he chose not to alter the narrative line, it was not possible for the sylphs to influence the action of the poem. The mock-epic joke is precisely how little real effect they have upon events. See Interpretations pp. 82–3 for further discussion.

Yet they are not without influence. Their affinity with the heroine is strong whether they are seen as images of her beauty and frivolous behaviour or as leading Belinda in the direction she wishes to go. She readily accepts the command *thy own importance know* (35), and this is the beginning both of her transformation to the status of a goddess and of her descent into self-inflated pride. (See Interpretations p. 97–8.)

13 **Sol** the sun
   white curtains probably the hangings around Belinda's four-poster bed rather than at the window.
13–14 In the 1712 *Rape* these lines read: *Sol thro' white Curtains did his Beams display/And op'd those Eyes which brighter shine than they.* Pope uses a standard literary cliché to praise Belinda's eyes, i.e. they shine more brightly than the sun. You might like to consider the differences between the two versions. Does the introduction of the phrases *tim'rous ray* and *must eclipse* sharpen a conventional image or has Pope altered our perception of the heroine? (For a further consideration of the sun image see Interpretations p. 111.)
15–16 The couplet makes two apparently unrelated statements but if lovers and lap-dogs wake at the same moment is some sort of parallel, however ludicrous, suggested?
   17 When Betty fails to answer the summons, Belinda impatiently knocks her slipper on the floor. The rhythm of the line echoes her irritation, with the caesura creating a pause in the middle before the quicker second half.

18 **press'd watch** the watch which she presses is a 'repeater', a fashionable and expensive type of watch made in London, which chimed to the nearest hour and quarters.

23 **Birth-night Beau** the festival held at Court on the evening of a Royal Birthday was called a Birth-night. Beaux would take pleasure in being glitteringly well-dressed for the occasion.

24 What causes Belinda to blush? There is no hint in the text. Pope, as so often in the poem, leaves it to our imaginations. Belinda herself is absolved of conscious awareness. After all, she blushes in a dream.

25 What meaning should be taken from *winning*? In the sense of the phrase 'winning ways' it means appealing or charming, a description of the surface attraction of the sylph Ariel. Is there a suggestion of another meaning, winning in the sense of gaining admisson to the bedroom, to Belinda's bedside while she sleeps? If so, who is winning and what is won? Notice that Pope starts the line with the word *Seem'd*, distancing himself. As so often with the innuendos, he disclaims authorial responsibility for the suggestive pictures he creates.

29 **infant thought** the first of several instances in which Belinda is likened to a child. Refer also to lines 31–32 and 37–40 and 89.

32 **silver token** silver coin. The belief that fairies leave gifts of money continues today. When children lose their baby teeth they often put them under the pillow at night, hoping to find in the morning that they have been exchanged for money.
circled green rings on the lawn supposedly made by fairies dancing in a circle.

33–34 These lines illustrate the Priest's teaching as the preceding couplet did the Nurse's. They refer to the Annunciation and the ways in which virgin saints were pictured.

35 **thy own importance know** 'know thyself' was the inscription at the Delphic Oracle, the shrine dedicated to Apollo at Delphi in Greece. The Oracle's answers were held by the ancient Greeks to be of great authority but were often very ambiguous. Ariel's advice neatly echoes and subverts this piece of wisdom. Is he encouraging Belinda to a just sense of her own worth or misleading her into the sin of Pride? The question of the importance of Belinda lies at the heart of the poem. How do you feel Pope judges her worth by the end of the poem?

37–40   These lines, together with those mentioned in the note on line 29, suggest that a quality of childishness is essential for the sylphs' protection to prevail. It allows us to see Belinda as either blamelessly innocent or childishly immature.

39   **Wits**   witty, showy, young men-about-town. See also *spark* (73).

42   **Militia**   troops

    lower sky   the space between earth and moon as distinct from the heavenly regions, also called the Lunar sphere because it is under the influence of the moon. See lines II 81 and V 113. Does the phrase imply the existence of a superior race of spirits who inhabit the higher etherial plane, perhaps the *wise Celestials* (77)? The idea is not pursued in the poem but Pope seems to be warning us not to take the sylphs too seriously. In spite of their airs and graces, of their claims to *contrive it all* (104), can they perform all they promise?

44   **Box... Ring**   a box at the theatre and the Ring in Hyde Park, a fashionable place around which to drive, and be seen driving, in a carriage.

45   **Equipage**   a private carriage and horses with attendant servants.

46   **a Chair**   sedan chair, carried by two men.

49   **transition**   perhaps an early reference to an idea that runs through the poem, that women's natures are changeable.

50   **Vehicles**   by using a heavy, trundling word as a metaphor for women's earthly bodies and a lighter word *Equipage* for their lives as sylphs, Ariel reinforces his claim that women move more freely and elegantly after their transformation. Is an airy existence more desirable than a human one? The choice between elegance and earthly passion is one which Belinda faces.

55–56   **Chariots... Ombre**   carriages were called 'chariots' at the time. *Ombre* is a card game, and is the game which Belinda and the Baron play in Canto III. Behind these *vanities* lies the echo of epic times when chariots carried heroes into battle and games were contests of physical prowess.

59–66   The four types of sprite which Ariel describes are based on the medieval belief that our physical bodies consisted of four base elements; air, fire, earth and water, and that human character was formed by whichever element predominated. For example, the spirits of fiery women are associated with salamanders, mythological reptilian creatures who, it was believed, could live in fire. Salamanders and nymphs disappear quickly from the poem; gnomes are reserved for the Cave of Spleen. Ariel's explanation concentrates upon the sylphs.

59 **Termagants** angry, scolding women, i.e. fiery.

62 **Tea** in the eighteenth century *tea* rhymed with *away*.

65 **Coquettes** young flirtatious women.

68 **embrac'd** taken in charge, protected. The offer of the sylph's embrace as a reward for remaining chaste, and the manner in which the structure of the couplet closely associates the alternatives, may hint at sexual undertones. If so, the following couplet could re-establish the innocence of the sylphs by stressing their disembodied natures. Or, bearing in mind how Jupiter, King of the Gods, transformed himself into different shapes in order to seduce mortals, it could be read as a vision of limitless pleasure. The lightness of tone (consider the cumulative effect of *sport and flutter* and *freed from mortal laws, with ease/Assume what sexes and what shapes they please*) seems delicately to keep these possibilities both open and unresolved.

72 **masquerades** masked assemblies and balls.

73 **spark** witty, lively, young man.

78 *Honour* this is the first mention of the word which becomes so significant as the poem develops. For a discussion of what the sylphs might intend by the term, see Interpretations pp. 83–4.

79 **too conscious of their face** too aware of their beauty.

81 **prospects** expectations of a titled marriage.

89 **bidden blush** a 'blush' created by make-up.

91–104 To describe the world of women as *mystic mazes* and a *giddy circle of vanities*, suggests that Pope considers women have no sense of purpose or direction. Yet he also refers to them as *tender* and *victim*. Is his attitude to their changeable natures critical or sympathetic? And if you feel that it is the latter, does this carry with it an element of patronage? (See Interpretations pp. 100–1.)

92 **mystic** although the adjective properly describes the mazes, is there a sense that the ways of women are mysterious to men? See also line 122.

94 **impertinence** silliness, foolishness, nonsense.

97–98 **Florio… Damon** standard literary names for lovers in light verse.

100 **Toyshop**   on the one hand the image asserts the essential
     instability and frivolity of women. (In the eighteenth century
     Toyshop referred to a shop selling trinkets, knick-knacks and
     fancy goods for adults.) On the other, it reveals the powerlessness
     of the sylphs who *shift* a heart which is already *moving*.

101 **sword-knots**   braided cord fastened to the handles of swords
     allowing the wearer to twist the cord around his wrist for security.

105 I, who claim to protect you, am one of these (sylphs). Pope's
     inverted syntax emphasizes Ariel's boast.

109 **impend**   approach.

110 **main**   the open ocean.

118–119 **Billet-doux**   love letter.
     Wounds, Charms, and Ardors   the language of eighteenth-
     century romantic flattery.

120 Visions and warning dreams are customary in epics and
     customarily vanish, but there may be a hint that the vision is
     lost because of Belinda's empty-headed nature. See also note on
     lines 91–104 above.

Lines 121–148

In a parody of the ritual of epic heroes arming for battle, Betty
helps to dress Belinda for an evening of coffee and cards at
Hampton Court. In the epic world this preparation often led to
death. Pope adopts the phraseology and solemn tone of the epic
(*Now awful Beauty puts on all its arms* [139]). Does some sense of the
gravity of the epic moment come across in these lines in spite of
the diminishing nature of the parallel with a young girl making-up?

The tone of the first bedroom scene, Belinda's awakening, is
mocking and suggestive. The blushes, the drowsiness, the
impatience, the ease with which she is distracted and flattered by
the conventional phrases of a billet-doux; all these make her
appear very young and human. In this passage the narrator's
attitude changes from one of amused indulgence to one of
adoration. We are witnesses to the transformation of Belinda
from an innocent girl to a goddess. (See Interpretations pp. 96–8.)

As well as echoing epic phrases, Pope uses religious imagery to create a tone which is awed and reverential, raising questions about the degree to which he is genuinely mocking. Worshipped and *deck'd with all that land and sea afford* (V 11) Belinda *arms* herself... for what? The question hangs in the air and like so many questions in the poem (*what strange motive... Was it for this you took such constant care?*) it is left hanging.

125–126   In *Paradise Lost* the newly created Eve glimpsed herself in a pool of water and fell in love with her image before she had set eyes on Adam or understood about reflections. Pope's allusion contrasts Milton's scene of pre-fallen innocence with Belinda's worship of her own reflection. However *heav'nly*, she knows full well whose image she sees in the mirror.

   127   **inferior Priestess**   Betty. The superior Priestess is Belinda who worships her own image in the glass.

   131   **nicely culls with curious toil**   selects precisely with attentive concentration.

   132   **spoil**   plunder, booty, valuables seized in war. Dryden used the phrase *glitt'ring spoil* in his translation of the *Aeneid* to describe armour which had been captured in battle. In the toilette *spoil* is reduced to jewellery and perfume. These are Belinda's *arms* (139), seductive weapons for the battleground of Hampton Court. However, the word *spoil* could suggest that the arms were acquired in a suspect, unearned manner. (For a further discussion see Interpretations p. 82.)

135–136   **Tortoise... Elephant**   Belinda's combs of *speckled* tortoise-shell and *white* ivory are examples of the idea of transformation which runs through the poem. (See Interpretations p. 101–3.)

   138   **Patches, Bibles**   patches of black material were worn by women on their faces as fashionable beauty marks. Small editions of bibles, no more than a few inches in width or length and elegantly bound, were produced in the eighteenth century for ladies to carry.

This famous line has been variously interpreted. Some critics feel that the word *Bibles* is incongruously slipped into the confusion of make-up and love letters to reveal the frivolous nature of Belinda's mind, unable to distinguish between things of lasting worth and things of the moment. Others have viewed the confusion of her dressing table as an imaginative profusion from which she arises, a newly created goddess. Critics who stress the economic basis of her adornment point to the resemblance between this line and mercantile lists of the eighteenth century which listed luxury objects indiscriminately. Products appeared in these catalogues because of their market value, not their moral worth. Then there is the question of the plurals. The likelihood is that the bibles are tiny. Could this be an accurate description of a young girl's dressing table with several elegantly small bibles lying there? What of the tone set by the alliteration and the movement from monosyllable to disyllables and a closing trisyllable? The way in which we read the line depends ultimately upon the way in which we view Belinda.

139 **awful**   creating awe. The long vowels *awe… all… arms* have a solemn sound. Do they suggest danger, a hint that Belinda's beauty may be a weapon in a battle yet to come? Or do you feel that they create a sense that Pope is in awe of the transformed Belinda?

143 **purer blush**   why should a blush applied by rouge be purer? The *bidden blush* (89) seemed to suggest a loss of innocence in *Infant cheeks*. Here Pope appears to favour a more sophisticated and refined beauty. Is he, as some critics have thought, falling in love with an artificial beauty he intended to mock?

143 **keener lightnings**   some form of eyedrop has been applied, perhaps belladonna which enlarged the pupils.

148 Notice how the tone which has remained grave, almost awed, throughout the passage is neatly undercut by the joke in the concluding line which returns us sharply from the altar to the boudoir. Pope apparently wants us to go out smiling.

Canto II: Lines 1–28

The verse paragraphs read like a swelling paean of praise to Belinda who *issues forth* from her toilette, transformed into a goddess rivalling the sun. Everything shines: the Thames, the nymphs and youths, her cross, her eyes and her ringlets. Surrounded by lesser luminaries as the sun is surrounded by comets, she is the undoubted centre of attraction. *But ev'ry eye was fix'd on her alone* (6). However, the word *But* which opens the line suggests that not all is quite as it should be. The couplets recoil upon themselves, hinting alternative readings. The mention of Jews and Infidels throws doubt on the religious significance of the *sparkling Cross*, which is worn presumably for ornamentation not devotion, and chosen to display wealth and beauty not faith. One of the best examples of Pope's skill at undercutting the apparent claims of his couplets is the presence of the word *unfix'd* in line 10. It returns the reader to line 9 and Belinda's *sprightly mind*. Are we to take *sprightly* as a compliment or not? In the sense of 'lively' it appears to praise Belinda but allied to *unfix'd* it implies that her attention darts from one thing to another in a shallow, scatty manner. (And what of the contrast with *fix'd* in line 6 to describe the devotion of her admirers?) As Pope's balanced couplets spring forward and turn back on themselves, one wonders whether to trust his first line or look for twists in the tail. How sincere, for example, do you find line 18?

2 **main** ocean.
3 **the rival of his beams** this is not the first time that Belinda has been compared favourably to the sun. (For a discussion of the sun image throughout the poem see Interpretations p. 111.)
7–8 The cross may serve to decorate the real object of adoration; *kiss* suggestively draws attention to her *white breast*.
11–12 Notice the antithesis of *none... all*; *Oft... never*. Do the words balance or cancel each other? You may feel they create a sense of a poised Belinda, smoothing over any possible offence with her smiles. On the other hand you might ask whether a smile is worth the favour she refuses to give.
14 **alike** another of those little twists at the end of the couplet which undermine the sense of what has gone before. Are we to take Belinda's liberality as evidence of her generosity of spirit or of her self-absorption?
15–18 **Yet... If** the syntax insists upon indecisiveness, balancing between admiration and mockery. See also *But* in line 6.

25 **sprindges**   snares for catching birds.
26 In Pope's time fishing lines were made of horse-hair. *Finny prey* is an example of what Pope called a diminishing figure. (See Interpretations pp. 104–5.) The ordinariness of the thing described, fish, is concealed by pompous language which indicates a lack of proportion in the poet's choice of words. The joke is created partly by the inappropriate use of language and partly by the sense that the characters in the poem are taking themselves over-seriously.

Lines 29–46

At this, our first encounter with the Baron, what portrait are we given? Homeric heroes such as Achilles, who killed the Trojan leader Hector in single combat, or Odysseus, who rescued his men from the Cave of the Cyclops by guile, were admired and renowned for *force* and *fraud*, but when these words are used of a *Lover's* exploits they smack of subterfuge and ravishment in a less than heroic sense. However teasingly the key term 'rape' is used in the poem, its primary meaning lurks beneath the jokes.

It is difficult not to sense ridicule in Pope's description of the ardent prayer. If the Baron can so lightly discard the intimate gifts of his former loves, what confidence have we that he will be any more steadfast in his new passion? Heroic language is used: *Propitious heav'n; trophies; the pyre; the Pow'rs gave ear;* and the hero's prayer before battle which the gods only partially grant was a standard epic device. But the overall tone of these lines mocks and belittles the Baron because his past behaviour appears so casually unserious.

35 *Phoebus*   the sun.
41 **pyre**   a pile of wood or combustible material, usually a funeral pile for burning a dead body.
45–46 These lines allude to incidents in the *Iliad* and *Aeneid*. Gods commonly granted only half the hero's prayer.

Lines 47–142

In these lines we have our first detailed picture of the sylphs and their contradictory natures, at one and the same time both colourful and nearly invisible. Their glittering appearances are vivid and elusive as their *fluid bodies* and *transparent forms* rapidly change and dissolve. Verbs of motion crowd lines 47–72. Many are intransitive, taking no object, perhaps suggesting that the restless movements reflect back upon the sylphs themselves. It is their own shapes and forms which are changed by this activity. Does it hint at a further idea, that their actions have little effect on anyone in the poem but themselves? (For a fuller discussion of the theme of change within the poem see Interpretations pp. 101–3.)

Like the Greek and Roman gods, the sylphs descend from their airy, upper world to intervene in the human sphere, adding to the poem that sense of the 'marvellous' which eighteenth-century readers expected in an epic, a sense that human destinies are ultimately controlled by supernatural forces who can arrange visions and visitations, appearances and disappearances, failures and victories with magical, divine power. By the addition of the sylphs (or 'machinery' as the supernatural element in an epic was known), Pope's protagonists lead their lives under the watchful care of divine beings. The difference with the mock-epic is that, for all their pretensions to power, the sylphs are powerless to control the action of the poem.

Notice how the military imagery which was introduced in Canto I, with the *light Militia of the lower sky* (42), continues in these lines. The *lucid squadrons* are commanded by a superior *chief* who exhorts them as before a battle, orders out a *special* patrol to guard the enemy's objective and punishes them for disobeying orders, *Whatever spirit, careless of his charge/His post neglects… Shall feel sharp vengeance* (123–125). The sylphs are warriors in Belinda's defence. The joke is that their willingness to defend may exceed Belinda's desire to be defended.

47 **secure** safely.

51 **Zephyrs** gentle winds. Zephyr was the classical Greek god of the west wind.

52 Belinda's smiles are associated with the warming and life-giving properties of the sun. Perhaps no other line in the poem so forcefully claims divine powers for her.

55–57 Notice the sibilants in these lines. They sound like the swish of silk or the feathering of wings.

55 **Denizens** inhabitants. In its literal sense, denizens refers to aliens who have been granted citizenship. Perhaps this is a glancing reference to the sylphs' previous existence on earth.

57 **shrouds** literally the ropes which haul the sails, but here the sails themselves.

70 **Superior** Satan in *Paradise Lost* is called *the superior Fiend* (Bk 1 283) in the sense of being the most exalted, the most important, which also applies here. Ariel is the *chief*, whom the aerial band must obey (73). The epic hero was naturally taller than his comrades. Ariel however owes his elevated position not to his physical stature, as did Satan or Achilles, but to his being perched on the mast-head.

73–90 Ariel addresses the band of sylphs with names which, taken from *Le Comte de Gabalis*, appear only at this point in the poem. Does this give you the sense of an innumerable band of troops ready to defend Belinda? Or does the roll-call of duties, on a cosmic scale and culminating in the defence of the British throne, mock the more trivial duties of the sylphs assigned to Belinda in lines 91–100?

77 **Æther** the purest aerial region, above the moon.

79 **wand'ring orbs** comets.

81 **less refin'd** the region between the earth and the moon, which was not considered as pure in nature as the celestial regions beyond the moon's influence.

86 **glebe** cultivated land; fields of corn.

88–90 The key commands *Watch... guide... guard* are placed at the climax of the verse paragraph. (For further discussion of the sylphs' duties see Interpretations pp. 82–3.)

91 **humbler province** after describing the celestial duties assigned to angels, *th'aerial kind*, Ariel comes to the significantly humbler tasks of the sylphs.

92 **pleasing... glorious**   the apposition of the two adjectives
suggests that one excludes the other. This may look forward to
the ending when Belinda's lock, transformed to a comet in the
celestial regions, *adds new glory to the shining sphere!* (V 142).
Belinda could be said to achieve glory at the cost of suffering
personal displeasure. Yet the tone of the poem accords more
with the first adjective than the second.

95 **vernal**   spring.

97 **wash**   cosmetic lotion.

100 **Flounce... Furbelow**   material gathered or pleated to form
borders for petticoats and dresses.

103 **slight**   trickery. The line echoes the Baron's determination to
win the lock by *force* or *fraud* (II 32).

105–110 These lines have been interpreted in various ways. Some readers
find Pope's teasing of Belinda and the disasters which threaten her
sympathetic and affectionate while others think he is being
ironically critical. Ariel predicts a series of *dire* events in a
balanced set of clauses which juxtapose the serious and the trivial
in a ludicrous mixture. For Belinda to lose her virginity is surely a
dire disaster, yet the balanced syntax of the closing line of the
couplet, placing the noun prominently before its verb, implies
that the sylphs value the China jar even more. In the following
couplets, one verb yokes together events of incomparably
different degrees of importance. Ariel's confused morality in
which virtue lies in unflawed appearances is mockingly revealed
and the lightness of tone suggests that Belinda shares the sylphs'
excessive concern with outward show. (See Interpretations
pp. 83–4 and pp. 107–10 for further discussion.)

105 *Diana*   Goddess of the moon, of hunting and chastity.
Breaking *Diana's law* meant to lose one's virginity.

110 Not for the first time there is a suggestion that Belinda's heart
belongs more to her lap-dog than to a man. It may be that the
fall of Shock, so plaintively predicted here, occurs during the
game of cards.

111–115 The sylphs' names derive from their duties. Zephyretta echoes
Zephyr, the gentle west wind; Brillante the look of jewelled ear
drops; Momentilla belongs to moments of time and Crispissa
to the crisping of locks. Does the sound of their names convey
a sense of their sylph-like qualities?

114 Belinda presumably wears her repeater watch hanging from her waist, which was the fashion of the times.

117 The 50 sylphs *of special note* are not mentioned again in the poem. Perhaps Pope highlights them to create a rhyme which throws *Petticoat* into prominence, for what is special is the petticoat itself. It is the citadel under attack and its close proximity hints that it is a symbol of her honour and a metaphor for her chastity.

118 **Petticoat** the fashion of the time was to wear a lower garment which was visible. Over it Belinda would have worn a loose dress or coat pinned back in front to reveal the 'petticoat'.

119 **seven-fold fence** the 'folds' are the layers of leather from which a Greek shield was made. Epic heroes customarily had shields fashioned from seven layers of leather. Achilles' shield was specially made for him by the god Vulcan who bound it with silver around the circumference. It was so famous that eighteenth-century readers would have had no difficulty in recognizing the allusion to it in Belinda's petticoat.

120 **hoops... whale** Belinda's petticoat is hooped and stiffened with whalebone.

121–122 Notice how the military metaphors delicately insinuate the underlying cause of the battle. As with the lock, Pope leaves the reader to decide the extent to which the Baron seeks articles of adornment for trophies and the extent to which they act as metaphors.

123–136 Given the sylphs' concern with appearances it seems fitting that their punishments should also lie in this field and that the instruments of restraint should be the very things they use as beauty aids when adorning Belinda. You might like to compare this passage with the scene in which Belinda applies her make-up (I 139–146). Notice how Pope's choice of words presents the same event in two different lights, the first a divine transformation; the second a torture chamber. The diminutive size of the sylphs and their desire to remain always on the wing is turned against them, amusingly so, if one visualizes the bodkin's eye and seas of frothing chocolate. Yet the language alludes to both Greek and Christian mythology; to Ixion and to Milton's Lucifer who had his flight restrained, imparting a note of grandeur to the mess of make-up and beauty aids. The verbs which limit their restless

47

movement: *stop'd, transfix'd, plung'd, wedg'd, restrain, clog'd*, reveal however another side to the ritual of make-up. The application of cosmetics was probably quite painful and some beauty aids, like those which contained white lead, were dangerous to health. The effort required to keep up appearances which is hinted at here will be developed more fully by Thalestris in Canto V.

126 **vials** small glass bottles.

128 **bodkin** a small tool made of metal or bone, usually, as in this line, a blunt-headed needle. The bodkin in Canto V with which Belinda attacks the Baron is a decorative pin fastening her dress and previously worn by her mother as a hairpin.

129 **Pomatums** scented ointments applied to the skin or hair.

131 **Alom stypticks** Alum is an astringent white mineral salt. *Stypticks* are substances which contract body tissue.

132 **rivell'd** contracted into wrinkles.

133 *Ixion* in Greek mythology, Ixion attempted to seduce Hera, the Queen of the Gods. Zeus, King of the Gods, forestalled and punished him by binding him to a fiery wheel which rolled unceasingly through the skies.

134 **Mill** chocolate, a fashionable drink at this time especially for women, was made by grinding cacao nuts and infusing the powder with hot water. The *whirling Mill* refers to the chocolate pot in which the powder was infused. A swizzle stick fitted into the pot through a hole in the lid and was rotated between the palms until the drink frothed.

139 **thrid** thread.

Canto III: Lines 1–24

The description of Hampton Court opens in epic style taking its syntax and vocabulary from Dryden's translation of the *Aeneid* and in particular from a passage about the walls of Carthage. For how long is the grand style maintained? By lines 9–18 are we not in the linguistic world of eighteenth-century society, where nymphs and heroes *taste* the *pleasures of a Court*? Pope's colloquial *and all that* has an easy, careless air. It is a lazy phrase which fits the indolent world of the beau monde. Perhaps the descent from high style starts with the use of zeugma in lines 6 and 8. (See Interpretations pp. 108–10.) Does the suggestion that the fall of tyrants and the fall of nymphs are of equal concern to *Britain's statesmen* mock the gravity of the scene so grandiloquently set forth in the first lines, or does it lend gravity to the 'fall' of nymphs and to Belinda's situation?

1   **meads**   meadows.

3–4   The palace at Hampton Court, built for Cardinal Wolsey in the sixteenth century and extended by Sir Christopher Wren in the seventeenth, was Queen Anne's favourite royal residence. It lay on the banks of the Thames, a few miles upstream from the City of London. The condition of the roads in the early eighteenth century meant that travel by the river was more practical as well as pleasant.

7   **three realms**   England, Ireland and Scotland.

8   A famous example of Pope's use of zeugma (See Interpretations pp. 108–9) in which a single verb takes two grammatically correct but stylistically incongruous objects. In the space of a single line the tone shifts abruptly and comically from the stately epic to the voice of a wit-about-town.

12   **visit**   an evening social visit. (See also the note on line 167.)

14   *Indian* **screen**   used to shield the direct heat of the fire and probably made of lacquer. At this time 'India' and 'Arabia' referred generally to the East. The screen could be from Japan.

19–24   This is one of the few moments in the poem when the daily life of the city openly surfaces and these famous lines have been variously interpreted. They are based upon a standard epic device for indicating that the time is evening by reference to labourers ceasing their daily work, but many readers have felt a cutting edge in the close of the couplet formed by lines 21 and 22. Pope's implication, that lives are being sacrificed for convenience, may horrify and could be taken as a serious criticism of the rituals of etiquette. The tone, however, is so elegantly mocking that one does not know whether to read the lines as unserious teasing or bitter satire.

23 **Exchange** in the eighteenth century businessmen did not work in offices as they do today. They transacted their affairs at coffee shops, many of which became associated with a particular branch of business, or at the Royal Exchange, which was a two-storey building in the City, a few streets to the north of London Bridge. It had arcades around an open courtyard where men gathered to do to business with each other.

Lines 25–100

The epic allusions are to sports contests where warriors competed at athletics and practised their battle skills, rather than to a battle. The imitation of an epic battle is delayed until Canto V, but do you feel a sense of a preliminary skirmish in these lines; a hint that the game of cards is either a screen or a metaphor for a sexual contest? The Baron's feelings are not disclosed. We see the game from Belinda's point of view and the language suggests a rising passion; *Burns to encounter, swells her breast*, but it is unclear to what extent she is aware of this herself. Is she innocent, naïvely flirtatious or aflame with desire?

26 **advent'rous Knights** the Baron was introduced as *advent'rous* (II 29). *Knights* may refer simply to the titled rank of Belinda's opponents but the word is suggestive of medieval tournaments with their air of mock battles. (See also the note on line 29.)

Is there also a pun intended, hinting a different kind of adventure?

27 **Ombre** a popular card game in Pope's time. It came originally from Spain (the name derives from the Spanish word *Hombre*, meaning 'man') and bears a resemblance to our contemporary game of whist. Nine rounds are played and to win a player needs to gain a majority of rounds or tricks. The third Knight is a necessary but shadowy character. Sometimes it is impossible to tell what cards he holds or plays. The contest is entirely between Belinda and the Baron. She must win five tricks to his four if she is to be the victor.

28 The suggestive phrase *swells her breast* implies that her *conquests* may not be merely at cards.

29–30 Each of the three players is dealt nine cards which make up the *three bands* of opposing warriors *in arms*. In spite of the epic allusion being to games on the sports field, the military metaphor is sustained throughout the contest, perhaps conveying a sense that not all the players are treating the game merely as a pastime. The *sacred nine* refers both to the number of cards each player holds and to the Muses, the sister-goddesses of arts and learning.

33 **Matadore** the aces, plus one other card depending upon which suit was chosen for trump.

37–38 Does the quirky, humorous quality of this couplet owe something to the odd alliteration, *four Kings… forky?*

41 **garbs succinct** short tunics.

42 **halberts** weapons which combined a spear and battle-axe on the same shaft.

44 **velvet plain** a phrase commonly used in pastoral and epic poetry to describe a green field. It refers here to the velvet-covered card table, but there may also be a sense of the plain or field of battle.

46 The line parodies the biblical phrase: *And God said, 'Let there be light' and there was light* (Genesis i 3). Although there is a ludicrous imbalance in comparing God creating light out of darkness on the first day of creation with a young girl declaring trumps in a game of cards, the comparison adds to the sense that, within the world of the poem, Belinda is a goddess. In one sense it shows the ridiculous heights to which pride has brought her, and sets her up for a fall. In another sense it continues the image which runs through the poem of Belinda as the sun, the light of the world upon which not only the Baron but all the *gazers* depend. *Belinda smil'd, and all the world was gay* (II 52).

47–48 **sable… swarthy** Belinda opens the game leading spades and clubs.

49 *Spadillio* Ace of Spades.

51 *Manillio* two of Spades.

53 *Basto* Ace of Clubs.

61 *Pam* Knave of Clubs.

62 *Lu* Lu or Loo is the name of a different card game in which

the Knave of Clubs is the most powerful card.

67 ***Amazon*** the Queen of Spades. In Greek mythology the Amazons were a tribe of warrior women.

69 Her first victim to die is the King of Clubs. The reversed syntax imitates the epic style.

70 **mien** features, expression.

71 **What boots** what helps.

76 **embroider'd** a common epic adjective. There is no sense intended of a piece of embroidery.

77 **refulgent** shining, gleaming.

80 **strow** strew.

87–92 Belinda's early success, easily winning four tricks in a row, appeared to put her in an unbeatable position. She needed only one more trick to win the game outright, and this is called *Codille*. However, the Baron wrested back the lead and took the fifth to eighth tricks. The game now stands at four tricks each. Everything depends upon who wins the final hand and Belinda *trembles* as she suddenly faces the prospect of losing a game which had seemed certainly hers. The sly references to the *wily* Knave and Queen of *Hearts* and the *shameful chance* at which the *virgin* blood forsakes her cheeks hint at more sensual reasons for her trembling. Hints are all we have. Pope delicately leaves the reader to judge the extent to which Belinda's passion is being aroused by the fear of losing at cards or winning at a quite different game.

96 **Trick** the Baron leads with the powerful Ace of Hearts but the winning card, the King of Hearts, is in Belinda's hand. Does any sense of trickery or cleverness on Belinda's part lie behind the surface meaning of the word *Trick*? She holds the King by luck but you may feel that *lurk'd* and *unseen* invest her playing with an air of cunning strategy. If so, does this increase for you the sense of her power or do you feel she is misled by a fortuitous win at cards into believing herself more powerful than she really is?

Lines 101–124

Epic warnings customarily told of mortal ruin and reminded heroes that their ultimate doom was certain. The lofty language and tone of lines 101–104 would not be out of place in an epic translation. Pope continues the high style in lines 105–112. Epic feasts were described in just such words in eighteenth-century translations. At what point does epic rhetoric and diction give way to the casual tone of eighteenth-century conversation? The brackets around the aside in lines 117–118 have the air of Pope nudging us and dropping a knowing remark into our ear. We are invited, by the colloquial tone, to share in court and coffee-house gossip. You may decide that phrases which point to the transition between the grandeur of the epic and the frivolity of eighteenth-century society appear even earlier. To which world do *the Fair* belong?

This passage is one of the occasions in the poem when the contrast in scale between the two worlds serves to magnify as well as ridicule and diminish. As with Belinda's toilette, the tone of grandeur and mystery created by such phrases as *crown'd… grateful… gratify… China's earth receives the smoaking tyde* seems to raise the act of drinking coffee to an elaborate ritual which Pope enjoys and reveres. Should readers share this admiration for the good things in life or take the lines as purely ironic? As so often, Pope seems to allow us to read the lines either way, or both at the same time.

106 Coffee berries were first roasted in a chafing dish on the sideboard (the crackling sound) and then ground in a mill.

107 Lacquer work from Japan began arriving in England from the East during the seventeenth century and small items of oriental lacquered furniture, such as chests, cabinets, screens and tables, were the height of fashion in Pope's time. The image of furniture as an altar at which this society worships was hinted earlier in the language Pope used to describe Belinda's toilette in Canto I. The tone here is similarly reverential. Lines 107–112

magnify the etiquette of coffee drinking into a religious
ceremony (*shining Altars... silver lamp... fiery spirits... silver
spouts*) and the act of worship is no longer private but
communal with overtones of nature's creative power. *China's
earth* (the cups) receives the *grateful* liquor. What are the
implications of *grateful*? Do you think that the adjective
transfers its sense to the thirsty participants or, as the grammar
suggests, the *earth*? The scale of the description is ridiculously
exaggerated, but do you detect irony in these lines? It may be
that some sense of the preciousness and beauty of these items
in the eighteenth century and in the world of the poem pulls
against the implied criticism of people who take social
ceremonies so seriously. (See Interpretations pp. 78–81.)

118 **half-shut eyes**   the apparent compliment to a politician's
wisdom (i.e. that with eyes only half opened he can see through
all things) is undermined by the ironic alternative meaning (i.e.
that his half-considered judgement is superficial and probably
wrong).

119 **vapours**   clouds of steam. The word appears innocent in this
line, referring to steam from the Baron's coffee. However, once
we reach the *constant Vapour* (IV 39) which fills the Cave of
Spleen and realize the undertones of ill-humour and disease
which accompany the vapours, we can recognize how deftly
Pope has amalgamated the literal sense of the word with its
poisonous and mischievous attributes.

122–124 In classical mythology, *Scylla* was the daughter of King *Nisus*
who, amongst his silver hair, had one purple lock of magical
power upon which the security of himself and his kingdom
depended. Scylla fell in love with her father's enemy Minos and
stole the lock to give to him. For this sacrilegious theft she was
rejected by Minos and turned into a bird. Like the reference to
Berenice's locks (V 129) this comparison highlights the
importance of locks of hair.

Lines 125–178

Though *two-edg'd weapon* (128) is clearly part of a cluster of battle imagery describing the Baron's attack (*stratagems* [120], *Knight* [129], *spear… arm… fight* [130]), it is less obvious that this phrase refers to a tiny pair of ladies' scissors. The distance in the comparison between scissors and a *spear* is ludicrously emphasized by the phrase *little engine on his fingers' ends*. The Baron is unable to fit his male fingers fully into the scissors. *Two-edg'd weapon* and *glitt'ring Forfex* are further examples of periphrasis (see the note on Canto II line 26) in which the ordinariness of the object is teasingly concealed behind somewhat mysterious and elevated epic phraseology. When Pope arrives at his final epic phrase, *fatal engine*, the seriousness with which we might regard the Baron's rape of the lock is undercut by the presence of an eighteenth-century voice, redolent of gossip and light-weight tittle-tattle. *Just then* (127)… *just behind* (133)… *A wretched Sylph* (150).

144 **lurking** why has Belinda used *all her art* to conceal from Ariel the idea of an earthly lover in her mind or heart? By refusing the sylphs' enticements to reject mankind (I 67–68) she loses their protection. Is there a sense of guile on her part? See also the note on line 96 on *lurk'd*. If you feel that this is so, do you think that Pope wishes us to approve or disapprove of her 'fall' from the sylphs' grace?

147 **Forfex** the Latin word for scissors, a deliberately pompous choice of a word rarely used even in the eighteenth century.

151–152 In Greek mythology, the Fates were three aged, blind goddesses who spun the thread of a man or woman's life. When the time came to end it, they cut the thread with shears. The sombre tone set by the allusion in the first line of the couplet is turned on its head by the airily dismissive tone of the concluding line. (See Interpretations pp. 106–7.) Is there the slightest of warnings that, while airy substances can escape Fate, mortals are more vulnerable? If you find this is an over-serious interpretation, in danger of spoiling the joke in this couplet, it

is still a point of view which appears with increasing insistence
in the remainder of the poem.

157–160 The reversal of the normal word order in this sentence sets the
high epic tone, a tone mockingly undercut by the juxtaposition
of husbands with lap-dogs and China vessels with the lock of
hair. In this confusion of emotion and morality where do
Pope's sympathies lie?

164 **Coach and six** a coach and three pairs of horses.

165 *Atalantis* refers to *Secret Memoirs and Manners of Several
Persons of Quality, of Both Sexes. From the New Atalantis, an
Island in the Mediterranean* by Mrs Manley. This was a salacious
book purporting to reveal contemporary scandals.

167–168 Evening visits, accompanied by servants bearing torches, were
part of the fashionable lady's social round.

173–174 The destruction of the towers and battlements of Troy, held to
have been built by the gods, was part of the revenge of the
Greeks on the Trojans at the end of their bitter ten-year siege
of the city.

Canto IV: Lines 1–54

Umbriel's visit to the Cave of Spleen is a mock allusion to
another epic set piece, the descent of the hero to the underworld.
The *gloomy Cave* is a *proper scene* for the Gnome Umbriel who is
described variously as *sooty, dusky, melancholy* and with *black
wings. The fair face of light* which his presence *sully'd* could well
describe the sylphs (do you recall the adjectives associated with
them? See Interpretations pp. 75–6) and the glittering world
which Belinda inhabits. With a smile Belinda makes her world
gay, whereas Spleen, a *wayward Queen*, lives in a *dismal dome.
Screen'd in shades from day's detested glare*, the *Goddess with a
discontented air* rules an underworld defined by contrast with
Belinda's shimmering daylight sphere; dark against light, black
against gold, sooty against gilded, gloomy against gay.

Pope draws also upon Ovid's *Metamorphoses* and upon a
description in that work of the gloomy cave where the goddess

Envy dwells. The *Metamorphoses* is a collection of stories about humans who were changed into natural forms: trees, flowers, animals, stars. In a similar way the Cave of Spleen is a place of transformations. Pope's description refers in lines 43–46 to the scenic transformations of contemporary theatrical illusions and scattered throughout the Cave are *Unnumber'd throngs of bodies chang'd to various forms* (47–8). Are we to take this perverse transformation of everyday objects, bottles and jars and teapots, as further proof of the ugliness of the Cave in contrast with the beauty of the world above? Or do the strangely altered shapes symbolize Spleen's power to transform the appearance and behaviour of women? She is pictured as a *wayward* goddess served by *Ill-nature* and *Affectation*. Umbriel openly boasts of how he helps to put women into bad-tempered moods which *spoil a grace*.

Lines 53–54 hint at more sinister, sexual undertones to the deformation of jars and bottles. Among the recognized symptoms of Spleen were hallucinations and delusions. Medical treatises described cases of patients who believed they had changed into familiar, domestic objects. Pope in a note to the 1736 edition of his *Works* claimed that he knew for a *real fact* a lady of distinction who imagined she was a goosepie. Beneath the nursery-rhyme humour of the oddity of the transformations in the Cave of Spleen lies a sense of frustration and repression (the *phantoms* and *dreams* of *hermits* and *expiring maids*), of neurotic fears and delusions breaking out in images of warped sexuality, which leave one wondering whether the passage is a compliment to Belinda or a warning of how she too might be transformed by Spleen. (See Interpretations pp. 89–94.)

1–2 Pope drew attention in the 1736 edition of his *Works* to the opening of the *Aeneid* IV where Dido, widowed Queen of Carthage, is falling in love with Aeneas against her better judgement. Dryden's translation reads:

> *But anxious Cares already seiz'd the Queen;*
> *She fed within her Veins a Flame unseen:*

Pope's concern that readers note the epic allusion raises questions. Is Belinda's anxiety and shame over her trivial loss diminished by the comparison with Dido's dilemma, torn between the love-longings of reawakened passion and the fear of putting herself and her kingdom into the hands of a stranger? Or does the tone of his lines echo the seriousness of the original, suggesting that Belinda too may be stirred by love-longings for the Baron, the *secret passions* which, as a virgin, she is less able than Dido to understand?

3–10 The passage builds to a climax through repetition and reiteration, the syntax of parallel clauses implying a sustained increase of intensity which collapses when we reach the pettiness of Cynthia's sulks after the generalized, sweeping claims of the preceding examples. As so often in the poem, unexpected shifts in style deflate the apparent meaning of the passage. The first line of each couplet could have come from an epic translation; the second line from lightweight contemporary satiric verse against women. Each couplet has a high/low, serious/mocking, male/female contrast. Note how the male/female antithesis within the couplets sets the frustration felt when an active, epic, male impulse is blocked against the frustrations of female passivity. Consider what this implies about the opportunities available to men and women and the different codes of behaviour expected of them. (See Interpretations pp. 100–1.)

4 Compare this line with Clarissa's warning, *she who scorns a man, must die a maid* (V 28). This is not the first time that the poem has hinted at lost opportunities. The nymphs, *too conscious of their face*, were destined for the *Gnomes embrace* (I 79–80), although what this fate entails is left vague in Ariel's soothing opening speech. The Cave of Spleen will paint a grimmer picture. If the words *rage, resentment, and despair* (9) suggest that a frustrated spinsterhood and hysteric old age are punishments for missed opportunities, how does this accord with the concern for Belinda's chastity which the sylphs, the symbolism and the narrative appear to stress?

8 **Cynthia** a common name for a nymph in contemporary romantic verse, both lyric and satiric. It derives from the Roman name for the goddess of the moon, viewed as sympathetic to lovers.

manteau   a loose upper garment worn by women, a type of coat swept back to reveal the petticoat beneath. (See illustration on p. 81.)

9   Glancing back to lines 3–7 one can see that each couplet in turn gives two instances of the hostile emotions listed here, the first an epic example, the second a contemporary one either elevated or diminished by the juxtaposition depending upon how the lines are read.

15   **proper**   personal, i.e. the place where he belongs.

16   *Spleen*   the organ called the spleen was believed to lie on the left of the body, thus *Pain* (24) stands at the goddess's side. Medical treatises, of which there were a great number by Pope's time since the disease had a long history, stated that it created vapours which ascended to the head, affecting the sufferer with headaches and melancholy. In Elizabethan times it was known as 'melancholy' and in Pope's time, as well as 'spleen', it was called 'hysteria', 'hypochondria' or an attack of 'the vapours'. This allows Pope to pun on the word *vapour* relating it both to the disease and to the clouds which surround Umbriel (18) and the goddess (59) and the Cave (39).

17   **pinions**   wings

18   **vapour**   a cloud of mist. The Cave of Spleen is wreathed in such mists. *A constant Vapour o'er the palace flies*, creating a fitting atmosphere for a diseased region which imitates the gloom of the classical underworld and the smoky depths of Milton's Hell. *Vapour* alludes also to the mists which accompany the visionary phantoms and the theatrical transformations (40–46). You may consider the mistiness of the scene adds to the sense that here things and people are transformed and not quite what they appear to be. Think about this in relation to lines 31–38 and 71–73.

20   **dreaded East**   the chill east wind was thought to provoke attacks of spleen.

24   *Megrim*   migraine, a severe headache. It was recognized that sufferers tried to avoid the light.

25   **wait**   wait upon, attend.

27   *Ill-nature*   what is the effect of associating ill-nature with a maiden old age? You might like to think about the picture of ageing which is presented here and in lines 29–38, and how it relates to Clarissa's speech in Canto V.

29–30 **pray'rs... lampoons** lampoons were cruel personal attacks in writing. Tillotson suggests that the prayers are in her hand because 'though damaging they are not as damaging as lampoons which are precious enough for an unpleasant person to store in the bosom'. The lines may however be metaphorical, suggesting that apparent devotion to the welfare of others is hypocritical since, in her heart, she is merciless.

31–38 *Affectation* a primary meaning of the word is 'a striving after, aiming at'. Pope personifies a feminine striving to remain sexually alluring in defiance of the passage of time. Although *diff'ring far in figure and in face* from aged *Ill-nature*, *Affectation* cannot be young. The roses of eighteen, it is implied, are due to rouge. Her *sickness* may be a pretence which allows her to receive visitors in what she vainly hopes is a seductive state of undress, but *sickly mien* rings true. A genuinely diseased air hovers over the passage.

39 **constant Vapour** see the note on line 18.

43–46 Theatrical illusions of this type were part of the contemporary stage effects, particularly in opera and pantomime.

43 **spires** coils.

46 **machines** stage machinery allowing angels to be suspended in air.

51 **Pipkin** small earthenware vessel.
Tripod a three-legged stand. Homer in the *Iliad* described a set of gold tripods made by the clever God of Smiths, Vulcan, which appeared to be self-propelled.

53 **prove with child** are pregnant.

54 The passage culminates in the most sexually allusive line of all. (See Interpretations pp. 91–4.)

Lines 55–88

Umbriel's request that Belinda be touched with *chagrin* follows an explanation of how irritation, or being *in a pett* affects women generally. It spoils their looks, it spoils their behaviour and, where their behaviour is beyond reproof, Umbriel deliberately creates false rumours to cause upset anyway. Whether in beauty or behaviour, the effect of chagrin is to *spoil a grace*. What qualities are being judged as graceful or graceless? Do you feel this is a male point of view or would you agree that it is a feminine fault to become ill-tempered over beauty blemishes? The phrase *to fifty from fifteen* has a light alliterative air, in keeping with the joking tone of the passage, but could the reference to women's sexually productive years suggest that the *vapours* have a serious basis in female physiology?

55 **past**   passed.
56 **Spleenwort**   the epic hero Aeneas carried a golden bough as a kind of passport when he descended to the Underworld. Umbriel imitates him by carrying a fern leaf of the plant spleenwort.
60 Hysteria was thought to have a positive, creative aspect which inspired poets as well as a destructive, delusionary effect.
64 **in a pett**   in a fit of ill-temper.
69 **Citron-waters**   alcoholic drink, a mixture of brandy and lemon rind.
71 **airy horns**   traditionally horns were the sign of a man who had an adulterous wife but *airy* means that in these instances the husband's fears are false. Umbriel is responsible for rumpling petticoats and tumbling beds, deliberately creating suspicion and havoc between husband and wife.
75 **costive**   constipated.
77 **chagrin**   ill-temper.
78 **half the world**   presumably it is the men, not the ladies, who would be upset by a sulking Belinda.
82 *Ulysses*   at the end of the ten-year siege of Troy, Ulysses, one of the Greek chiefs, was fated to wander the seas for a further ten years before he could return home to his faithful wife Penelope. On his voyages he stopped at the island belonging to Aeolus, Warden of the Gales, who made him a present of a leathern bag in which were imprisoned all the adverse winds.
85 **Vial**   small glass bottle.

Lines 89–140

Belinda is dejected by the loss of her lock but neither aroused nor angry until Umbriel opens the bag of discontented winds over her head. Thalestris's speech increases her fury. Does this go any way to excusing her behaviour in Canto V?

What picture of beauty is given by the words *durance, bound, tort'ring, strain'd, bravely bore the double loads of lead*? These images of Belinda being imprisoned and tortured by her beauty-aids are similar to those Ariel threatens the sylphs with in Canto II 123–136. There the tone was humorous; here you may sense a more serious air. Of the two pictures we are given of Belinda's toilette, in Canto II and Canto IV, which do you find the more realistic, which the more truthful? (And are these necessarily the same?) The point of the self-inflicted punishment is raised but the question, *Was it for this… ?* is left for the reader to answer.

Thalestris makes much of the *unrival'd shrine* of Honour at which, she claims, *all* is resigned. What sort of honour can be lost *in a whisper*? Is Thalestris using the word in the same sense as the sylphs in Canto II when they set out to guard Belinda equally against a stain on *her honour* or her *new brocade* (II 107)? Like the sylphs, she appears to equate appearance, the reputation for virtue, with the real thing, but does Pope and should Belinda?

89 **Thalestris** Queen of the Amazons, in Greek mythology a race of warrior women.
92 **vent** opening.
99–101 These lines paint a picture of the trouble it took to create ringlets and locks with curling papers. *Fillets* were head-bands sometimes made of metal.
106 Is *all* meaningless or a revealing slip of the tongue?
114 **Expos'd thro' crystal** the Baron plans to wear the lock in a crystal ring, set with diamonds, which will allow the hair to show through the clear glass.
117 **Hyde-park Circus** the fashionable drive in Hyde Park. (See also the note on line I 44.)

118 **Bow**   St Mary le Bow was the traditional centre of the
mercantile City of London. Being born within the sound of
Bow bells identified one as a local, as opposed to the more
fashionable West End where wits would expect to live.

124 **nice conduct**   neat flourish.
clouded cane   streaked or mottled walking stick.

137 The Baron's grand claim will be ironically fulfilled in Canto V
when his *vital air* is blocked by a sneeze caused by the snuff
Belinda throws at him and he indeed loses the lock.

Lines 141–176

Pope models Belinda's lament on a famous passage in the *Iliad*
where Achilles mourns his fallen friend Patroclus. Pope's tone is
that of a young coquette complaining (*and* Shock *was most
unkind!*). Where he borrows language from the epic (*For ever
curs'd be this detested day*) Belinda's distress seems humorously
exaggerated. At other points the exaggeration creates a sense of
innocence. Is it likely she would rather have remain'd *un-admir'd*
especially in *some lone isle?* She seems very young in these lines.
Not to know *what mov'd her mind with youthful Lords to roam* is to
retreat to childhood. And if we feel that she could, on reflection,
answer her own question, would she have spoken the final
couplet if she had realized the sexual *double-entendre* it contained?

156 **Bohea**   an expensive variety of tea.

162 **patch-box**   the patches worn by women as fashionable beauty
marks were kept in ornamented boxes.

164 **Poll**   Belinda's parrot.

175–176 The reader is expected to recognize that Belinda is offering to
sacrifice the essence of her virtue for its outward appearance.
The question is whether she herself realizes the implications of
her words. Are they spoken knowingly, echoing Thalestris's
claim in line 106, or do they establish her essential innocence
and youth?

Canto V: Lines 1–102

Clarissa claims that her advice to Belinda (to strive to be *first in virtue* as she is in *face*) is common sense. With the loss of beauty comes the loss of power over the opposite sex. It is *good sense* therefore to *preserve what beauty gains* by *charms* which are more lasting.

Eighteenth-century readers would have recognized that Clarissa's speech was modelled on Sarpedon's call-to-arms in the *Iliad*. Pope had translated and published this famous episode before commencing his full translation of the *Iliad*. See Appendix 3 for Pope's translation of the speech. In his speech the epic hero Sarpedon inspires his companion Glaucus by comparing an honourable and valiant death in battle with an ignoble old age. Although we are expected to see a mocking contrast between courage in the face of death and good humour in the face of decay, you may feel that some of the grandeur of the original passage is caught in the tone of these lines.

Pope did not add Clarissa's speech to *The Rape* until he published the third version in 1717. He claimed that he did so 'to open more clearly the MORAL of the Poem'. Some readers see Clarissa as the moral centre of the poem, but not all do. Others argue that the conclusion proves that Belinda wins more by passion and pride than she would ever have achieved by remaining placidly good-humoured. And many regard the poem as a joke which requires no moral. There remains critical disagreement about Clarissa's speech. Does it encapsulate, change or avoid the moral of the poem? Or is *The Rape* an affectionate and teasing picture of a day in the life of a belle which we misread if we search seriously for a moral?

2 **Jove** the Roman name for the King of the Gods, also known as Jupiter or, in Greek mythology, as Zeus.
5–6 **the Trojan** Aeneas who, urged by the gods, abandoned his lover *Dido*, Queen of Carthage, and continued on to Italy to fulfil his destiny of founding Rome. When Dido saw Aeneas's

men preparing a fleet of ships and guessed that he was about to leave her, she broke out in furious accusations. Her speeches failed to alter his resolve so she sent her sister Anna to him with tearful but equally fruitless messages.

14 **side-box** box at the side of a theatre.

17 **front-box** the front-boxes in a theatre were nearest to the stage and set at an angle which gave the audience a clear view of whoever sat in them.

20 **small-pox** a highly contagious and often fatal disease until Jenner's discovery in 1796 of the cowpox vaccine. If victims survived the attack they were left disfigured, their faces pitted with pock marks. In the eighteenth century it was sufficient to have a clear complexion to be considered a beauty. The poem's obsession with cosmetics glosses over a reality which surfaces here, reverberating with warnings in spite of the light tone. Is it, after all, *a sin to paint?*

A particular pang may have been felt by those intimate with the Petres and Fermors because Lord Petre died of the smallpox in 1713, two years after the first version of the poem and four years before Pope added Clarissa's speech.

23 **patch** (see the note on line I 138)
   ogle glance flirtatiously.

35 **no applause ensu'd** if Clarissa's plea to value good humour and good sense above charm and beauty is indeed the moral (see the general note on lines 1–34) then, within the poem, it falls on deaf ears. And any certainty that Pope intends such a moral to be taken, if not by Belinda at least by the reader, is belied by what happens finally to the lock and to her name in lines 149–150.

37 **Virago** a female warrior.

40 **whalebones** used to stiffen women's clothing, particularly undergarments, such as corsets and girdles.

42 **base** bass.

44 **mortal** is the wound mortal because it is fatal or because it is inflicted and sustained by men as opposed to gods? The first meaning mocks the bravery of *Heroes* who battle against *fans* and *whalebones*: the second has sexual implications, the wounds of human passion.

47 *Pallas* Pallas Athene, Goddess of Wisdom.

    Mars   God of War.

    Latona   goddess mother of Apollo and Diana.

    Hermes   messenger of the gods.

48 *Olympus*   Mount Olympus in Greece was believed to be the home of the gods.

50 *Neptune*   God of the Sea.

53 **sconce**   wall-bracket to hold candles, often backed with a mirror to increase the light by reflection.

55 **bodkin**   these useful instruments, either needles or decorative pins (see lines 88–96) are here transformed into spears, emphasizing the diminutive nature of the sylphs and also their intrinsically domestic concerns.

59 **Witling**   a fop possessed of little wit.

60–66 The beaux (no longer referred to as heroes, but given the names of foppish characters, such as *Dapperwit* and Sir *Fopling Flutter*, from Restoration comedies) 'die' with phrases from theatre and opera on their lips. The romantic clichés contrast with the epic language of lines 45–52 and the seriousness with which the fops take themselves is mocked by the descent from grand, heroic phraseology. The sexual meaning of the verb 'to die' (for males, to achieve a climax and lose arousal) suggests that the sexual battle is real. Is there also a literary joke; an implication that the wits' metaphors and songs are full of borrowed, hackneyed phrases and second-hand language because their wooing is insincere and unoriginal?

65 *Mæander*   the name of the river echoes the verb 'to meander' or wander slowly.

66 **Swan**   refers to the poetic legend that swans sing once only, at the moment of death.

68 *Chloe*   a common name for belles in light poetry.

69–70 Note how Sir Plume goes down a *hero* but rises again as a *Beau*. Is this another example of the mocking juxtaposition of epic and colloquial styles or is there a sexual connotation in the revival of a lover?

73–74 **beam**   the crosspiece of the scales from which are suspended two pans in which the wits and the hair are weighed against each other. Do you think the barely perceptible difference in weight compliments Belinda or equates her lock with the wits which have been discredited in the previous lines?

77–78 If the fight were primarily a show of physical strength *unequal* would be a strange adjective since the sense clearly indicates that it is Belinda who is the stronger opponent. All is explained by the second line of the couplet where the Baron's desire to make love to Belinda is clear. In the sense of 'only', *no more* shows the inherent weakness of his position. His will waits upon her agreement. Is there another meaning to *no more*, an ironic sense that *more* than this he could not hope for?

82 **Snuff**   tobacco in a finely powdered form which was sniffed up the nostrils. The pinch of snuff which Belinda throws at the Baron causes a sneeze that completely subdues him.

88 **deadly**   after stressing the minuteness of the bodkins used by the sylphs as spears, can Pope intend this word seriously?

Lines 103–150

Images and themes which run through the poem come to their culmination in the concluding lines: the sun image, the transformations, the allusions to myths and legends about people translated at death into heavenly bodies. Do you feel a sense of melancholy in these lines; an admission that underlying the exaggerated claims for Belinda's beauty there always lay an awareness of its transience? Is this balanced by the promise that her lock and her name will survive? Or does the reappearance of the Muse show us that Pope believes the true source of glory is neither Belinda's beauty nor her lock, but his poetry?

91 **seal-rings**   rings with engraved stamps on their faces which were used to impress a pattern on sealing wax to seal a letter or validate a legal document.

105 *Othello*   in Shakespeare's play of the same name, the hero Othello is driven distracted by jealousy of his innocent wife Desdemona. A crucial element in the false accusations brought against her by his evil lieutenant, Iago, is a precious handkerchief which Othello gave her as a love gift. There are several speeches in the play which express his distress including one where he falls into an epileptic fit.

109 **guilt... pain** *force* or *fraud* (II 32), *force or slight* (II 103), *stratagems* (III 120) and *mischief* (III 125) have all been associated with the Baron's rape of the lock. This is the first suggestion of guilt or pain.

113 **Lunar sphere** the airy region which lay between earth and moon (and below the eternal sphere) was under the influence of the moon. It was inhabited by the sylphs (II 81) and filled, if we are to believe the description of the following lines, with the discarded trivia of the beau-monde, along with items which hint at the falsity of human emotion and the waste of human endeavour.

117 **alms** gifts or money for the poor. The implication in *death-bed alms* is that miserly people give only under the fear of damnation.

122 **tomes of casuistry** unreadably long books of dull, scholarly argument.

125–126 Romulus, the legendary founder of Rome, was translated to the heavens at his death, appearing in a vision to Proculus.

129 *Berenice's* **Locks** a figure in classical legend whose locks were similarly turned into stars.

133 *Beau-monde* the social world of beaux and belles.
Mall a tree-lined avenue beside the royal palace of St James, a very fashionable place for walking, driving or playing Pall-mall, a kind of croquet.

135 *Venus* Goddess of Love.

136 *Rosamonda's* **lake** Rosamond's pond in St James's Park was a notorious meeting place for lovers.

137 *Partridge* published almanacks annually in Pope's time making ridiculous predictions which never failed to include the downfall of the Pope (*the fall of Rome*) and the King of France (*the fate of Louis*).

138 *Galilæo's* **eyes** Galileo was an Italian astronomer of the late sixteenth and early seventeenth centuries, who was an early inventor of telescopes.

139 **egregious** absurd.

Interpretations

Genre: epic and mock-epic

Pope called *The Rape, an Heroi-comical poem*, by which he meant a mock-epic. He could assume that his eighteenth-century readers, educated in the classics and knowledgeable about epics, would recognize that it was a mockery. Many of his jokes rest upon this assumption. For the modern reader, notes identifying the sources of his parodies are helpful, but a better way of appreciating the humour of his exaggerated style is to read, even in part, translations of the classical Greek epic, Homer's *Iliad*; or the Roman epic, Virgil's *Aeneid*; or the English epic, *Paradise Lost* by John Milton.

Epic subjects were grand: the Trojan wars, the founding of Rome, the fall of Man, and were narrated at length in twelve or more books, each consisting of several hundred lines. The epic hero traversed a wide geographical area over a long period of time, encountering battles, romances, journeys by land and sea, even a descent into the underworld. From on high the gods watched the human drama, intervening when they chose. Success for the hero was dependent upon the subplot of divine intrigue as well as his own courage and skill. His fate was ordained. Honour, the epic ideal, lay in journeying on, fighting bravely and accepting whatever end the gods had willed.

The form and style of an epic was so clearly recognized in Pope's time that he teasingly drew up a set of rules for aspiring epic poets 'without a Genius, nay without Learning or much Reading. This must necessarily be of great Use to all those Poets who confess they never Read, and of whom the World is convinced they never Learn'. He published the following spoof (*The Guardian* 10 June 1713) in the manner of a cooking recipe.

A Receit to make an Epick Poem
>   Take out of any old Poem, History-books, Romance, or Legend...
>   those Parts of Story which afford most Scope for long
>   Descriptions: Put these Pieces together, and throw all the
>   Adventures you fancy into one Tale. Then take a Hero, whom you
>   may chuse for the Sound of his Name, and put him into the midst
>   of these Adventures: There let him work, for twelve Books...

He continues in the same mocking manner, laying down rules for
writing descriptions,

>   Pick a large quantity of Images and Descriptions from Homer's
>   *Iliads*, with a Spice or two of Virgil,

and choosing language,

>   Here it will do well to be an Imitator of Milton, for you'll find it
>   easier to imitate him in this than in any thing else.

The mock-epic, also an established literary form in Pope's time,
imitated the most recognizable aspects of the epic, its form and
elevated language. It used an inflated style to ridicule the
pretensions and pomposity of minor quarrels. It exposed the
limitations of contemporary society by the implicit contrast with
an expansive epic world. The idle pursuits of the beau monde
and the low pursuits of the inner city were shown to be
unworthy of a literary form firmly associated with heroes.

At the same time as he was writing *The Rape*, Pope was
engaged in translating Homer's *Iliad*. Translations of epics were
highly regarded and better paid than original poetry. Pope was
financially so successful in his venture that he went on
to translate Homer's *Odyssey*, albeit with the help of
unacknowledged contributors. He read widely in earlier English
translations of Virgil and Homer and from these he borrowed
elaborate phrases for *The Rape*. He borrowed from *Paradise Lost*.
Again and again Pope's language would not be out of place in a
serious epic. The joke lies in his applying this elevated style to

'the life of modern ladies in this idle town' as he deprecatingly described the subject of *The Rape* in a letter to a lady friend.

The opening

Homer set the pattern for epic openings in the *Iliad*. This is Pope's translation of the opening lines.

> Achilles' Wrath, to Greece the direful Spring
> Of Woes unnumber'd, heav'nly Goddess, sing!

The subject of the poem is announced immediately. This is called the 'proposition'. The poet then calls upon a goddess or muse to inspire his song. This is the 'invocation'. For added emphasis normal syntax (the word order of the sentence) is reversed. Object precedes verb, and the object of the verb is the subject of the epic.

Activity

In a similar style Virgil commences the *Aeneid*. Here is Dryden's translation which Pope knew well. Can you identify the proposition and discover who the poet calls upon for inspiration?

> Arms, and the Man I sing, who, forc'd by Fate,
> And haughty *Juno's* unrelenting Hate;
> Expell'd and exil'd, left the Trojan Shoar;
> Long Labours, both by Sea and Land he bore;
> And in the doubtful War, before he won
> The *Latian* Realm, and built the destin'd Town:
> His banish'd Gods restor'd to Rites Divine,
> And setl'd sure Succession in his Line:
> From whence the Race of *Alban* Fathers come,
> 10 And the long Glories of Majestick *Rome*.
> Oh Muse! the Causes and the Crimes relate,
> What Goddess was provok'd, and whence her hate:
> For what Offence the Queen of Heav'n began
> To persecute so brave, so just a Man!
> (*The Poems of John Dryden* ed. Kingsley, 1958)

Discussion

The proposition of the epic is *Arms, and the Man*. The opening paragraph describes his deeds and from these clues a contemporary reader would recognize him as Aeneas who, driven from Troy, founded the *destin'd Town* of Rome. The poet calls on the Muse to relate the story, as though he could not do it without her aid.

The subject of the poem, *Arms, and the Man*, is placed before the verb *sing*, of which it is the grammatical object. This is a reversal of the normal word order of the English sentence; subject, verb, object. In the same way Milton turns the long opening sentence of *Paradise Lost*, with an even greater distance between the main verb and its object. Can you identify the subject of the poem and the main verb of the sentence?

> Of Mans First Disobedience, and the Fruit
> Of that Forbidd'n Tree, whose mortal tast
> Brought Death into the World, and all our woe,
> With loss of *Eden*, till one greater Man
> Restore us, and regain the blissful Seat,
> Sing Heav'nly Muse, that on the secret top
> Of *Oreb*, or of *Sinai*, didst inspire
> That Shepherd, who first taught the chosen Seed
> In the Beginning how the Heav'ns and Earth
> 10 Rose out of *Chaos*: Or if *Sion* Hill
> Delight thee more, and *Siloa's* Brook that flowd
> Fast by the Oracle of God; I thence
> Invoke thy aid to my adventrous Song,
> That with no middle flight intends to soar
> Above th' *Aonian* Mount; while it persues
> Things unattemped yet in Prose or Rime.
> And chiefly Thou O Spirit, that dost preferr
> Before all Temples th' upright heart and pure,
> Instruct me, for Thou know'st; Thou from the first
> 20 Wast present, and with mighty wings outspred
> Dove-like satst brooding on the vast Abyss

And mad'st it pregnant: What in mee is dark
Illumin, what is low raise and support;
That to the highth of this great Argument
I may assert Eternal Providence,
And justifie the wayes of God to men.
  (*The Poetical Works of John Milton*, ed. Helen Darbishire, 1958)

Milton's syntax follows the pattern of the opening of an epic. He announces this poem's subject in the first line (*Mans First Disobedience, and the Fruit/Of that Forbidd'n Tree*) but the main verb *Sing* is delayed until line 6. The remainder of his long sentence is given over to subordinate clauses describing the Christianized muse whose aid he invokes (13) and (22–23) and who is the subject of his main verb.

Pope consciously imitates the epic opening in his first twelve lines. He too will *sing* (3) his subject whose importance he indicates by inverted syntax and elevated language: *dire offence, mighty contests, tasks so bold*. He invokes inspiration. He addresses the muse. His tone has the declamatory epic ring as he commands the goddess, *Say what strange motive* (7).

At some point, and not too far into the poem, you should sense that Pope is mocking the epic form, laughing at his subject. Try reading the first three paragraphs (1–26). Can you find a moment when you felt the poem might be a joke? For me it is the idea of sleepless lovers who do not wake until noon.

Once we realize that we are reading a mock-epic, it casts a different light on the apparent solemnity and dignity of Pope's proposition and invocation.

Activity

Read Canto I 1–12. Can you identify any departure from the conventional epic opening or any hint of mockery in these lines?

Discussion

It seems that the first hint of the mock-epic comes in line 3 where Pope credits a human rather than the muse with inspiring his poem.

The ambiguity of *ev'n Belinda* has been mentioned (see Note to I 4). With lines 5–6 we can be more certain. Epic causes may be amorous or trivial; epic subjects are never slight. From then on Pope's irony becomes clearer. Words appropriate to different and conflicting spheres of action appear together; *well-bred lord and gentle Belle* belong in the drawing room; *assault* on the battlefield (or in the back-alley?). Their inappropriate juxtaposition suggests mockery while leaving open the question of what is mocked. The implications of lines 9–10 are that the Belle is self-interested, not heroic. And can we take Pope seriously when he asks in the elevated language of the epic *whether tasks so bold* are fit for *little men*?

Finally there is the matter of tone. Pope's opening has an easy tone compared to Dryden or Milton's weighty words and learned references. Perhaps the ultimate distinction between epic and mock-epic is the contrast in the attitude of each poet to his task; Milton's humility, *What in mee is dark/Illumin, what is low raise*, and Pope's elated claim, *Slight is the subject, but not so the praise*.

The setting

A glittering world of wealth

The setting of the poem shimmers with wealth. It depicts a world of luxurious things: silks, watches, gems, snuff-boxes, fans, caskets, canes, screens, mirrors, vases, chinaware. The lives of Belinda and the Baron are cosseted by rich objects and the adjectives associated with them add to their lustre: *gilded, silver, sparkling, speckled, gilt, shining, rich, painted, glitt'ring.*

What should we feel about this accumulation of wealthy possessions? The atmosphere created by the adjectives might suggest that Pope delights in the exquisite craftsmanship and beauty of precious objects. In phrases such as *gratify their scent and taste* (III 111) and *beauty draws us with a single hair* (II 28) he appears to share his characters' enjoyment of fine things. Other phrases however are more critical of their pampered lives.

The *instructive hours* spent at court are passed in *various talk*

(III 11) which Pope refers to a few lines later as *chat*. What sort of learning is summed up in the word *chat*? And what are the implications of the closing phrase of the couplet:

> Snuff, or the fan, supply each pause of chat,
> With singing, laughing, ogling, and all that.   (III 17–18)

The dismissive tone of *and all that* implies that Pope is judging the *instructive hours* and finding them wanting, in both educational and moral terms. (The adjective *instructive* is a change Pope made from *the chearful hours* of his earlier version). Similarly there are moments when Pope appears to mock his characters' possessions and it is difficult to know whether his attitude is indulgently teasing or highly critical. Many of the poem's phrases show Pope balancing delicately between disapproval and delight.

Activity

How effectively does Pope portray the Baron's altar to love (Canto II 37–43)?

Discussion

It is built of *twelve vast French Romances, neatly gilt*. What are the connotations of *vast*? The adjective may refer to the physical size of the books (but should romances be so weighty?) or their length (are these books unreadably long?). *Vast* could mean intolerable or magnificent. The tone seems to be simultaneously hostile and admiring. And what of *gilt*? The word appears to stress the books' value and attractiveness but equally the neatness of the gilt might suggest that they have never been opened, let alone read. And how great is the sacrifice of a broken set of garters or gloves?

Bright inhabitants of the air

Precious possessions are not the only things which glitter in the poem. There are also the iridescent, shimmering sylphs.

Activity

Read Canto II 59–72. How does the language suggest a connection between the sylphs and the material objects in the poem?

Discussion

Some of the words in the passage (*gold, glitt'ring, richest, gilded*) are adjectives which Pope used of the wealthy setting. Their presence here suggests that the sylphs too are part of the poem's glittering ambience, reflecting and contributing to the radiant atmosphere. Other words stress their *half-dissolv'd, filmy, transparent* forms and their restless movement; *waft, fluid, loose, disports, colours that change*. If you concentrate upon these words the sylphs appear thin and insubstantial beside the solidity of chariots and barges, snuff-boxes and coffee pots. They share the colours of the earthly world but lack its substance; e.g. the shears which sever Belinda's locks have no effect on the sylphs because *airy substance soon unites again* (III 152). The thinness of their glitter is even clearer if you compare them with the human protagonists. They lack warmth. They are unmoved by the desires which inflame Belinda and the Baron and, at the climax, they are powerless in the face of passions they do not possess. Their fluid, transparent qualities may be a hint that their powers will fade away when confronted by the reality of warm human emotions.

Beauty and fragility

A significant numbers of things in Belinda's world are expensive and beautiful but also delicate, fragile and easily broken. Three times in the poem the fragility of china is mentioned:

Or when rich *China* vessels fall'n from high,	
In glitt'ring dust, and painted fragments lie!	(III 159–160)
Or some frail *China* jar receive a flaw	(II 106)
The tott'ring China stood without a wind	(IV 163)

Like the cracking of delicate chinaware, brocade can be stained, necklaces lost, petticoats fail and a lock of hair vanish. Everything precious is vulnerable. Perhaps it is an essential quality of preciousness. What does this suggest about the most precious thing in the poem, Belinda herself?

When her toilette is completed and her beauty is at its most flawless, Belinda issues forth to rival the sun. With all the hints about the vulnerability and fragility of precious objects, are you surprised to find that in spite of her own efforts, Betty's efforts and the sylph's efforts *frail beauty must decay* (V 25)? Clarissa spells out the fate which beautiful girls share with precious possessions: *painted, or not painted, all shall fade* (V 27). Nothing saves them from the ravages of time.

Activity

Read Canto II 105–110. Compare what happens to objects and what happens to young girls.

Discussion

The incongruity of the pairings gives a ridiculous air to the lines, creating a joking tone which suggests that the events are accidental and should not be taken seriously. Perhaps it strains against the laughing mood of the passage to point out the obvious, that, for most people, the loss of virginity and the chipping of china are events of incomparably different orders of seriousness. The passage can be read as teasing mockery which has no intention of making reasonable sense. It could be a comment (affectionate or ironic or critical) on a world of style where values belong to appearances and where good taste and polite behaviour are as important as honour and chastity.

The juxtaposition of material accidents and moral failings could imply a connection as well as an ironic contrast between china and chastity. Cracked vases, stained brocades and lost necklaces are images of Belinda's chastity which the critic Cleanth Brooks (1943) compares to fine porcelain, 'brittle, precious, useless and easily broken'. You may argue that, far from being useless, Belinda's innocence is part of her seductive appeal for the Baron but is it ridiculous to equate a young girl's virginity with objects of rare and delicate fragility?

The mercantile background

So far we have considered objects as though they operated in the poem as part of the background to Belinda's world or as poetic images. But these objects were also real artefacts in the lives of a wealthy section of society. Take, for instance, the three familiar beverages consumed in the poem: tea, chocolate and coffee. These entered England in the mid-seventeenth century as an experimental addition to the East India Company's cargoes of silks and spices. Coffee houses started up in London in the late seventeenth century and by the time of *The Rape* they had become fashionable rendez-vous for business men. Tea trickled in more slowly. Sales expanded significantly only at the beginning of the eighteenth century when its high import duty was reduced. Pepys mentions in his diary drinking his first 'Cupp of Tee' in 1660 and the drink was so new that it was spelt variously as tee, tay, and tea, tcha, cha and chaw. Coffee drinking was normally a public occasion; tea was considered a ladies' drink and served privately, although Queen Anne offered it as an evening entertainment at Hampton Court.

In the eighteenth century, as England became a powerful trading nation, the effects were evident in the variety of merchandise available. In the *Review* January 1706 Daniel Defoe describes the expansive reach of English trade.

> What a Quantity of the *Terra Firma* has been carried from *Newcastle* in *Coles*... Tin, Lead and Iron... These we carry abroad, and with them we purchase and bring back the Woods of *Norway*; the Silks of *Italy* and *Turkey*; the Wines and Brandies of *France*, the Wines, Oil, and Fruit of *Spain*; the Druggs of *Persia*; the Spices of *India*; the Sugars of *America*; the Toys and Gaiety of *China* and *Japan*.

Addison in *The Spectator* May 1711 shows patriotic pride when he visits London's trading centre, the Royal Exchange.

> There is no Place in the Town which I so much love to frequent as the *Royal-Exchange*. It gives me a secret Satisfaction, and, in some

measure, gratifies my Vanity, as I am an *Englishman*, to see so rich an Assembly of Country-men and Foreigners consulting together upon the private Business of Mankind, and making this Metropolis a kind of *Emporium* for the whole Earth... Our Ships are loaden with the Harvest of every Climate: Our tables are stored with Spices, and Oils, and Wines: Our Rooms are filled with Pyramids of *China*, and adorned with the Workmanship of *Japan*: Our Morning's-Draught comes to us from the remotest Corners of the Earth: We repair our Bodies by the Drugs of *America*, and repose our selves under *Indian* Canopies. My Friend Sir ANDREW calls the Vineyards of *France*, our Gardens; the Spice-Islands our Hot-Beds, the *Persians* our Silk-Weavers, and the *Chinese* our Potters.

An eighteenth-century print of the Royal Exchange in the City of London. See Canto III 23

In the eighteenth century, drinking chocolate was made by dissolving ground cacoa beans in water in a mill (see above). As a final touch the hot drink was frothed by hand. The swizzle stick fitted through the hole in the lid and was twirled between the palms. See Canto II 133–136

In the same essay, Addison describes a fashionable lady's dress such as Belinda might have worn as the *Product* of world-wide mercantile trade.

> **The single Dress of a Woman of Quality is often the Product of an hundred Climates. The Muff and the Fan come together from the different Ends of the Earth. The Scarf is sent from the Torrid Zone, and the Tippet from beneath the Pole. The Brocade Petticoat rises out of the Mines of Peru, and the Diamond Necklace out of the Bowels of Indostan.**

A manteau, pinned up
at the back in the
fashion of the time to
reveal an underskirt
or petticoat. See
Canto II 118 and
Canto IV 8

Activity

Read Canto III 105–118. What do you think the attitude of
contemporary readers would have been to the things Pope describes?

Discussion

When infusing coffee is exaggerated into raising *fiery spirits on Altars
of Japan* and cups turn into *China's earth*, the tone sounds pompous
and mocking. But the status of tea and coffee drinking at that period
could account for the description seeming almost reverential.
Eighteenth-century readers would recognize the silver lamp, Japanese
lacquer and China porcelain as expensive, exotic, imported
commodities. Most of the objects in the poem are modish, stylish, costly
items of conspicuous consumption. This throws a somewhat different
light on the sylphs, trembling lest Belinda spill coffee on her brocade.
She is adorned with *Unnumber'd treasures* and *various off'rings of the
world* (1 129–130). The labour which created, the merchants who
transported and the wealth which paid for the things which deck her
are not mentioned directly, yet it may be that Pope is not altogether
mocking when, a few lines later, he calls her beauty *awful*.

At the toilette Betty arrays Belinda in glittering *spoil*. What does the word convey to you? One of its primary meanings is the loot which marauding armies seize. To make off with whatever he could carry was a victorious soldier's right. In this sense Belinda's lock can be seen as battle-spoil; as the gain which the conquering Baron will seize upon. The aggressive and military language used for his designs (*By force to ravish, or by fraud betray* [II 32]) suggests a commander plotting a campaign. Thalestris refers to the lock (IV 113) as *th' inestimable prize*. The lock can be read as a metaphor for the lady and the decking of Belinda in spoil may suggest that she herself is the prize.

If, however, we treat the lock as spoil in the mercantile sense it implies an article chosen carefully with an eye to its economic value. Belinda rises from her toilette a finished product, an object of desire. Luxury objects are desirable because they confer status on the possessor. Has Belinda become a 'thing' to be owned and displayed? Is she prized because she is beautiful, expensive, precious and, once possessed by a man, a sign of his conspicuous consumption?

The sylphs

The sylphs are Pope's mocking re-creation of the gods who watch over the heroes of epics and guide their fortunes. It is nicely fitting that Pope's supernatural beings, who are supposed to imitate Homer's deities and Milton's angels, are tiny, frail and powerless. Far from taking a decisive part in the action, these flimsy creatures are afraid of human men. *An earthly Lover lurking at her heart* (III 144) is all it takes to frighten them away. Although they are an amalgam of epic machinery, Rosicrucian lore (see Notes I 13–120) and English folk tale, they are essentially Pope's invention. As Dr Johnson pointed out, we need no background information to picture them.

A race of aerial people, never heard of before, is presented to us in a manner so clear and easy, that the reader seeks for no more information. (*The Lives of the Poets*, 1781)

Activity

How would you describe, or draw, a sylph? Which phrases best capture the essentials of their appearances?

Discussion

I see them as small, winged creatures, like iridescent dragonflies. They are *ever on the wing* (I 43); they *flutter* (I 66) on *insect-wings* (II 59) and their fluid forms are *transparent* (II 61) to the reader (*tho' unseen* [I 43]) by humans in the poem. *Thin glitt'ring textures of the filmy dew* (II 64) or *half-dissolv'd in light* (II 62) are key phrases for me. How tiny they are! They even seem to diminish in size as the narrative continues. Ariel hovering over Belinda's head in Canto I was a favourite scene with the poem's illustrators. In the eighteenth century they tended to depict him as a winged Cupid, in the nineteenth as a fairy doll, but always of sufficient size to be clearly visible. Yet in Canto II fifty sylphs are required to surround Belinda's petticoat and in Canto III one thousand close in to protect her lock.

Their duties are solely concerned with female adornment and female behaviour, both of which are portrayed as elegant and graceful like the sylphs. There is no equivalent machinery to guard or guide the men in the poem. Why do the women alone require protection and what are we to make of this indication of their fragility and weakness? Is Belinda's status enhanced by the presence of a troop of celestial beings whose entire *raison d'etre* is to perfect and protect her appearance, or do the sylphs suggest a trivializing and enfeebling concern with her own attractions?

The sylphs of course take their duties seriously. Is the joke against them for attempting to assume the epic role in a society devoted to leisure or can they justify the moral tone of the language? They use the high epic term *Honour* (I 78) as though it were synonymous with themselves.

Activity

Read Canto I 67–104. What do you think is meant by Ariel's use of the word 'honour'?

Discussion

The word honour is elusive and undefined in the poem. Honour – or sylph – (syntactically the words are interchangeable) *guards the purity* of maids. To equate it baldly with virginity loses the seductive charm of the passage. These Maids are *melting* (71) with *warm desires* (75). They court sexual encounters at balls and masquerades and the sylphs' protection does not inhibit such encounters but encourages and increases them. The sylphs claim to be on the side of virginity; *whoever fair and chaste/Rejects mankind, is by some Sylph embrace'd* (I 67–68) but women who refuse proposals and deny love are predestined for the *Gnomes embrace*. Where do the sylphs stand?

Thalestris uses the word *Honour* to mean reputation. To her, Belinda's honour is irretrievably lost with the visible loss of her lock and the Baron's display on his finger. The outward sign is all. The sylphs, for all their concern with appearances, seem genuinely interested in Belinda's innocence. The language of Ariel's warning suggests she will not *victim fall* (I 95) in spite of her warm desires because the sylphs can divert her attention with childish delights; *treat* and the *moving Toyshop of the heart*. She is a tender maid, poised between childhood and womanhood. Her position is delicate because her innocence and youth, as well as her warmth and beauty, are part of her attractiveness. Honour may be a matter of clinging to the rules of behaviour until she is more experienced in the ways of men, and the presence of the sylphs could be a sign of her acceptance of these conventions of polite manners.

Pope slips the word *unfix'd* into his tribute to Belinda's beauty (II 1–18) to describe her sprightly mind. *Unfix'd* captures an essential quality of the sylphs, with their *fluid bodies* (II 62) and *colours that change* (II 68), able to assume *what shapes they please* (I 70). Like them, Belinda is physically radiant and like them her moods vary and her emotions flutter. You could see the changeable nature of the sylphs as symbolizing the fluctuating emotions of a girl on the brink of sexual awakening.

84

Belinda embarking for Hampton Court, surrounded by cherubic sylphs, 'fair nymphs'and 'well-drest youth'. An eighteenth-century watercolour by Thomas Stothard

Belinda at her toilette, with Shock, Ariel, fairy sylphs and a bat-like creature, perhaps escaped from the Cave of Spleen. An unsigned nineteenth-century sketch, probably by Benjamin West or William Locke

The game of cards

The game of Ombre which Belinda plays with the Baron and a third unidentified knight is somewhat like modern whist or bridge. Three players play nine rounds or 'tricks' and the winner is the one who takes the most tricks. To win, a player must either win five tricks against an opponent or four tricks if the two opposing players win three and two respectively. However the strength of the cards differs from those in modern games. Belinda leads from her strongest to her weakest; the Ace of Spades is the strongest trump, then the two of Spades, then the Ace of Clubs, then the remaining trump suit in descending order down to the three of Spades. Red Aces are lower in value than any face card in their suit.

The basic rules are:

---

1 Remove from a deck of cards all eights, nines and tens, leaving forty cards.
2 Deal nine cards to each player and place the remaining cards face down in a pile.
3 Once trumps are decided, players may exchange their weaker cards with those in the pile.
4 The player who declares trumps (the challenger) plays the first card.
5 Each player plays one card in turn and the strongest card wins the trick.

Activity

With the help of the Notes for III 27–98 see how many of the remaining spaces you can complete in the plan of the game, given below. Pope does not give us sufficient information to complete the plan entirely but it is possible to decide who wins each trick.

The Game of Cards

Trick	Belinda	The Baron	Lord Anon.	Winner
1	Ace of Spades	A lesser Spade	A lesser Spade	Belinda
2				
3	Two of Spades		Card of little value	
4				
5		Queen of Spades		
6				
7				
8				
9				

You may have found the exaggerated language of the mock-epic contest complex and inexplicable at first reading. Has replaying the card game helped you to distinguish between words which are unusual because they belong to the terminology of eighteenth-century card games and those which are an imitation of the grand epic style? Even at his most exaggerated, Pope bases his parody on the real game being played by the contestants while subtly hinting that the game may not be solely about who wins at cards. Pope's attitude to the underlying sexual nature of the contest is conveyed in asides (*oh shameful chance!* [III 88]) and in his description of Belinda's behaviour. Why does he emphasize that the blood forsakes her *virgin's* cheek; why make her exultation so excited?

Activity

Re-read III 47–100. Can you find words which are both mock-epic and a realistic description of the game of cards?

Discussion

The *sable Matadores and swarthy Moors* (47–48) *Asia's troops, and Afric's sable sons* (82) refer to the black suits; the King of Spades' *manly leg* (57) and the King of Clubs' *globe* (74) reflect the way in which these figures are represented in their full-length pictures on the faces of the cards; the *verdant field* (52) and *level green* (80) are both the grassy sports arena and the green baize or velvet card table.

The Cave of Spleen

Pope's descriptions of luxurious things create a gilded setting for his poem. However, there are moments when the comfortable tenor of the elite, aristocratic life is disturbed and we glimpse a dark abyss. The Cave of Spleen is an underworld of pain and despair. And what of the couplet dropped, apparently casually, into a mock-epic description of the approach of evening, *The hungry Judges soon the sentence sign,/And wretches hang that jurymen may dine* (III 21–22)? In the City of London, there were eight annual Sessions at the Old Bailey where felons were tried and could be condemned to death and these Sessions could last from 6.30 am until 9 pm. Jurymen were chosen by the Sheriff from those citizens who possessed a freehold in land worth at least ten pounds per annum. In 1680 Sir John Hawles published a pamphlet *The Englishman's Right* which justified and praised *The Excellent designed use of Juries.* Hawles warns jurymen against agreeing 'blind fold' with long-standing members, 'Antient Jurymen' who rashly deliver their Opinions in order, amongst other reasons, not to spoil dinner.

> 'Tis frequent, that when Juries are withdrawn that they may consult of their *Verdict*, they soon forget that Solemn Oath they took... Presently the F*oreman* or one or two that call themselves *Antient* Jury-men (though in truth they never knew what belongs to the place more than a common *school-Boy*) rashly deliver their *Opinions*, and *all the rest* in respect to their supposed *Gravity* and *Experience*, or because they have the biggest *Estates*, or to avoid the trouble of *disputing* the Point, or to prevent the spoiling of *Dinne*r by delay, or some such *weighty* Reason, forthwith *agree blind fold*, or else go to holding up of hands or telling of *Noses*, and so the *Major Vote* carries away *Captive* both *Reason* and the *Conscience* of the rest.

The pamphlet was reprinted many times in the eighteenth and nineteenth centuries. We can glide over Pope's lines as a mock-epic joke, but contemporary readers might register them more ironically. Do these lines, even in joke, reveal a brutality held at bay by exclusiveness?

The Cave of Spleen makes it clearer that Belinda's world is not secure. It is filled with grotesque objects making it a favourite subject with illustrators of the poem.

Activity

Compare the three illustrations of the Cave on pages 91–93. Consider similarities and differences in the artists' choice of objects and how closely they follow the text of the poem.

Discussion

Certain objects seem to catch the imagination of artists. The Goddess Spleen dominates. Handmaids are always present and living teapots, maids turned bottles and the talking pie (which changes from a goosepie to a gooseberry pie over the years.) Beardsley has a strange interpretation of *Men prove with child* as he delicately outlines a foetus in the swollen belly of one of his male figures and in the thigh of another. The sexual implications of the maids who call for men to cork their bottles is illustrated by Du Guernier who places men's heads in the bottles. By contrast Wale in 1757 has female heads in the bottles. Pope's couplet:

> Unnumber'd throngs on ev'ry side are seen,
> Of bodies chang'd to various forms by Spleen.   (IV 47–48)

invites artists to fill the Cave with their own designs. Beardsley takes advantage of this. At the centre of his Cave, he places a recognizable drawing of Pope, copied from a well-known portrait by Kneller. This may be a tribute to the poem's author, or perhaps an acknowledgement that Pope himself suffered greatly from headaches and knew the melancholy which arises from pain and sickness.

The Cave of Spleen by du Guernier, one of the etchings which illustrated the 1714 edition of *The Rape of the Lock*. The hand maidens, Affectation and Ill-nature, attend the Goddess Spleen, while sooty Umbriel flits through the mist above living teapots and bottles corked with men's heads

The Cave of Spleen by Samuel Wale, an etching from the 1757 edition of Pope's collected *Works*. Ill-nature and Affectation stand behind the goddess, with Pain at her side and Megrim at her head. Umbriel hovers above a living teapot, bottles corked with maids' heads and pie through whose crust poke a head and webbed goose foot

The Cave of Spleen by Aubrey Beardsley, a photogravure illustration to *The Rape of the Lock* (1896). Umbriel and the Goddess Spleen dominate this gathering of fantastical creatures (some not mentioned in the poem). Along the lower edge stand pregnant men, living teapots and a tiny gooseberry pie, while in the centre is a portrait of Pope

The various illustrations of the Cave catch its air of theatrical unreality and also of diseased disorders.

As images of abnormal procreation, repressed sexuality, neurotic anxiety and frustration, the deformed objects present an unappealing picture of a life in the *Gnomes embrace* (I 80). Spleen was a recognized disease at the time with a long medical history pertaining to both men and women. It is noticeable that in Pope's Cave it is women who are affected by it. Are we seeing the disease, a form of hysteria and depression created by repression and despair, from a male point of view which relates it primarily to female sexual disorders? Are we to take the peevish, ill-natured, affected women depicted here as a warning of what life could be like for Belinda if... what? If she becomes a Prude? Or remains a coquette? Or are these ills the inevitable consequence of ageing? All these possibilities are hinted at in the contrast between the underworld of the Cave of Spleen and the golden, glittering world of Belinda's sun.

The Baron

In 1706 Pope wrote in a letter to Walsh: 'Monosyllable-Lines, unless very artfully managed, are stiff, or languishing: but may be beautiful to express Melancholy, Slowness or Labour'. Does this remind you of any lines in *The Rape*? Sir Plume, in nearly four consecutive lines of verse, speaks 26 monosyllables lightened by only three non-monosyllabic words, and two of those are weak feminine rhymes: *devil/civil* (IV 127–130). *Stiff* and *Laboured* exactly describe his manner, in contrast to the Baron's elegant, witty joke, expressed in a single, lengthy, balanced sentence (IV 131–138). One feels that the Baron's ironic reproof, enjoyed by the reader, passes over Sir Plume's head.

Activity

Do you think this is the same effete hero we met in Canto II?

Discussion

The syntax of lines II 30–3, unencumbered with adjectives or adverbs, and the rapidity with which the three verbs in line 30 follow each other fit the image of a decisive *advent'rous* man, but *force… ravish…* and *fraud* disturb this idea. What image of manliness is presented here if the Baron's battle honours are *trophies of his former loves?* Is he regarding Belinda as merely another trophy? (Note the hunting as well as military connotations of the word.) It is difficult not to sense ridicule in Pope's description of his ardent prayers. Is this in any way softened by the verbs in lines 35–43 and the phrases *tender Billet-doux and empty air*? However in Canto IV the Baron speaks well and gains in stature in his exchange with Sir Plume.

Pope mocks the Baron, but he presents him as a sophisticated gentleman. (Lord Petre was the head of one of the pre-eminent aristocratic Catholic families in England.) As today, there was at the time concern that tea and coffee were dangerous stimulants. Pamphleteers warned against them as intoxicating drugs. Surely

Pope is joking when he writes that coffee fumes make politicians *wise*, yet *vapours* are blamed for sending new stratagems to the Baron's brain, leading him to break the bounds of polite behaviour as Belinda has already done with her exultant shouts. Does Pope really believe that coffee fumes are dangerous, or are they a hint of something else?

The nature of the encounter between Belinda and the Baron is made clear in the *double-entendres* in Canto V, some blatant (78, 98, 102), some more ambiguous (44, 67–70). Belinda appears still to regard the contest as a struggle for the lock, but the Baron is well aware of what he has lost by his earlier attack. Not he but *some other* will win the lady. What commenced as trophy-hunting has turned into true passion. There is a real sense of loss in his speech *Boast not my fall* (97–100) from a man who claims he *sought no more*, in whichever sense we choose to read that double-edged phrase. Do you find your attitude softening towards the Baron as he reveals himself susceptible and vulnerable? Has he become victim rather than aggressor? Or are we being invited to view both him and Belinda as victim and aggressor at the same time?

Belinda

As she drowsily and reluctantly awakes Belinda seems very human. Of course she is pampered, protected by her wealth in a world where *wretches hang*, but she is also a young girl dreaming romantic dreams. By the end of the first Canto she has been transformed into a goddess. She emerges at the start of Canto II adorned, adored and divine.

Activity
What techniques does Pope use to suggest that Belinda is divine?

Discussion
There seem to me to be at least four ways by which this is established. First, the female sex is regarded with reverence throughout the poem.

Hailed as *the Fair* (II 91) and *Angel-like ador'd* (V 12), they are guided through the world by attendant sylphs. Secondly, from these belles Belinda is especially singled out as the *Fairest of mortals*, the *distinguish'd care* of the bright inhabitants of air (I 27). Thirdly, imagery confers upon her life-giving, divine power. From the moment of her awakening she is associated with the sun, the timorous *Sol* (I 13). Three times in the first paragraph of Canto II she is compared to the sun and Pope claims that she equals him in glory. The gazers depend upon her for life-giving sustenance (II 13); the gaiety of the world derives from her smile (II 52). Finally we, the readers, witness the moment of her transformation.

Belinda's toilette is the climax of Canto I. Indeed it is one of the climaxes of the poem. It is organized into three sections, starting at *And now... Unnumber'd treasures... Now awful Beauty* (I 121–148) and each section uses a cluster of images to exemplify its central action.

Activity

What is happening in each section? Can you identify a phrase or an image cluster which sums up the action?

Discussion

The first section (see Notes on Canto I 121–128) shows Belinda seated at her dressing-table admiring herself in the mirror. This simple action is presented as an epic parody and as an act of religious worship. The phrase *sacred rites of Pride* seems to me a central image from which the other images flow. They are all taken from the ritual of worship; like an inner shrine the *Toilet* is *unveil'd* and the words of devotion continue: *mystic order, rob'd in white, adores, Cosmetic pow'rs, heavenly Image, inferior Priestess, altar's side*. Belinda is both Priestess and Goddess, worshipping herself in a *rite of Pride*.

The second section (see Notes on Canto I 129–138) lists the objects on her dressing table and the central image seems to me to be *glitt'ring spoil*. The world has been ransacked to adorn Belinda. However conscious we are of the diminishing effect of the epic parallel (see Notes I 132), the tone does not seem entirely mocking. *India's glowing gems... All Arabia breathes* lend a radiance to

Belinda's beauty which enchants and the array of her dressing table seems to be gifts for a goddess. Some commentators believe that Pope came to mock but stayed to adore. Others have suggested that the lines reflect the glow of eighteenth-century male pride in Belinda as a created object of desire because she is decked in the fruits of their mercantile success.

In the third section (see Notes I 139–148) Belinda is made-up and her hair and gown are arranged. The effect of imagery may be less apparent here until you consider the verbs: *puts on, rises, repairs, awakens, calls forth, arise, quicken*. These are all words of creation. Belinda is born anew, transformed by the sylphs from a natural girl into a goddess who will rival the sun. Is her beauty natural or acquired? The verbs *awakens* and *calls forth* suggest that her latent good looks are merely heightened by make-up but *purer blush* and *quicken* suggest that the sylphs have added something which did not previously exist.

She reigns, a Queen commanding her troops, until the Baron cuts off her lock. How does she behave then? She *screams* (III 156), she *shrieks* (III 157), she collapses into *tears* (IV 144). With drooping head she signs for *my best, my fav'rite curl* (IV 148). Does this sound like a goddess or a retreat into childishness? At the end of Canto V the sun image reappears to spell out the truth of Belinda's situation. She is human, not divine. She may, in the lightweight language of coquetry, *slay millions* but in reality her *fair suns shall set*.

The movement of the poem can be read as an elevation leading to a fall. *Thine own importance know* the sylphs urged, and pride betrays Belinda into believing that her power is limitless. The toilette which transformed her was called *the rites of Pride*. At times the language echoes Milton, recalling Satan and Eve and the Biblical Fall. Mirroring this, Belinda's pride changes to despair and her guardianship moves from the sylphs to the gnomes. Belinda appears privileged but fragile. At what cost, at what effort her beauty is maintained! Is fear the underlying reality of her world? Fear of a fall, fear of growing old or of growing ugly, of losing the power to attract men? Is the fragility of her world the result of tension and anxiety engendered by the battle with time? She strives to keep up appearances and nature and youth are on her side but this will not always be so. As Belinda's glories come under attack, her passion and panic mount.

Coquettes and prudes: Thalestris and Clarissa

Coquettes charm and conquer men while refusing to capitulate to them. The Cave of Spleen hints that the end of their existence is *Affectation*, the vain striving to maintain power once beauty has fled. Prudes on the other hand retain their independence from men by disdaining the sexual battle altogether. *Ill-Nature* may personify their destination. Belinda has the beauty to be a coquette while maintaining her petticoat as a *seven-fold fence*. Does she seek power over men by remaining unavailable?

After death *light Coquettes* (I 65) transform into sylphs while gnomes were once Prudes. As long as Belinda is under the care of the sylphs, she too is a light coquette, besotted with chariots, balls, visits, card-playing and above all, her own appearance. When desire for a lover betrays her into the Gnomes' embrace she becomes a fiery termagant and then a prude wishing she had *stay'd... at home* saying her prayers and denying to herself that she ever wanted to *roam* with *youthful Lords* (IV 159–160).

The narrative line of the poem opposes the Baron to Belinda but some critics feel the conflict is really between Belinda on one side and Clarissa and Thalestris on the other. Ultimately Belinda and the Baron want the same thing, a sexual encounter, whereas Thalestris (and the sylphs) fight to keep Belinda a coquette, a pure object of desire. '*Was it for this...?*' she asks of the effort that has gone into manufacturing Belinda's beauty, and the rhetorical question appears to insist on the answer 'No'. But if not for *this* then why did Belinda take such care with her appearance? There is another answer which is in the affirmative: it was precisely for *this*, for attracting and arousing men.

In her generous plea to *keep good-humour still, whate'er we lose* (V 30) Clarissa can be seen as the heroine of the poem, the only character who successfully translates the epic concept of honour to the contemporary scene. In the world of belles, honour becomes the courage to face decay with good humour and a duty to *use* the power of beauty *well*, although what is meant by those elusive words is left for the reader to decide. Alternatively, she can be seen as the voice of experience, teaching Belinda with a knowing air how to hold on to a man. Do you find her advice moral or practical? Is she wise or worldly wise? The unanswered questions pile up (9–14) and it is worth trying to answer them for this will help you to decide what Clarissa means by her final warning, *well our pow'r to use*.

Clarissa seems less a prude than an aging coquette. Some view her critically as opportunistic and cunning, self-righteously lecturing Belinda on the way to retain adulation when beauty fades. Or is her advice the tactical compromise of common sense, soothing Belinda's anxieties that there will be loss if she gives way to her desires, a loss imaged in the stains and cracks which so concern the sylphs? To the sylphs honour means purity, whether in a vase, a dress or a woman. Beauty must be flawless and they admit of no discrepancy between appearance and reality. To Thalestris honour means reputation, the outward sign. Does Clarissa offer a third definition – honour as good-humoured, patient acceptance (of men? of marriage? of spinsterhood?) instead of despair before the inevitability of change?

If so, this draws attention to feminist readings which see Belinda as diminished by her experiences. Such readings regard the poem as dominated by a male point of view in spite of Belinda being the subject. In this interpretation women become objects for men's use, trophies or commodities, and they are judged as using their power *well* when they accept gracefully the social place which has been defined for them by men. Feminist critics consider Belinda loses her autonomy in the course of the poem, dwindling into a subdued, self-denying wife. You may feel that Pope, marginalized by his deformities and his religion, shows more sympathy with the position of women in eighteenth-century society than this view allows but it is worth thinking about the extent to which Belinda's power is dictated by the willingness of men to be attracted.

Other critics believe the positive tone of the key words in Clarissa's speech: *preserve, gain, produce, use, power, prevail* show Belinda being inducted into socialized womanhood. The poem is an 'attempted enlightenment in which a beautiful self-centred girl can become a superior communal woman' (Weinbrot 1997). Is Clarissa trying to educate Belinda kindly in the ways of good behaviour which will ensure her place in genteel society? Spence recorded Pope as saying, 'True politeness consists in being easy oneself and making everybody about one as easy as we can. But the mistaking brutality for freedom (for which many of our young people of quality in particular have made themselves so remarkable of late) has just the contrary effect.' As a young person of *quality*, has Belinda been allowed too much freedom?

Transformation and change

In Canto I 47–50 Ariel explains that after death women's souls transmute into their first Elements. What type of aerial being might Belinda become? In the course of a day we see her change from soft nymph to serene goddess to light coquette to fiery termagant to melancholy child. Her character is *unfix'd* and the poem leaves her at the close the same malleable young girl we met at the opening. She cannot remain a belle for long. The fragility of her beauty has been imaged in the fragility of the precious objects. If she is not to become a sylph or a gnome or any of the characters in the Cave of Spleen, what should she do? By the end she has experienced the results of unrestrained passion, been showered with advice and urged towards restraint, good humour and polite behaviour. Will she change? Should she?

Activity
Find two things which transform in the poem and consider whether the change is for better or for worse.

Discussion
Many things change. Epic language magnifies simple things: scissors become a two-edged weapon, bodkins become spears, all Arabia is contained in a box, a girl is transformed into a goddess and a lock into a star. The language seems to enhance the original object. Then there are the mock-epic diminutions when Gods dwindle into sylphs and heroes become little men. There are the natural changes brought by time as dresses are stained and curled locks turn to grey. There are unnatural changes in the Cave as bodies are *chang'd to various forms by Spleen*. These changes are for the worse.

Cracked china and flawed jars suggest that Belinda's loss of virginity is a real loss, a flaw in her beauty. Yet the apotheosis of the lock would not have taken place had Belinda stayed at home or followed Thalestris or Clarissa's advice. And are these Belinda's only options? Can we be certain that marriage is the goal Clarissa advocates? What if marriage were the loss Belinda has to face? (If you are interested in this idea you might like to read a poem Pope published in the same miscellany as *The Rape*: *To A Young Lady, With the Works of Voiture*. It echoes much of Clarissa's advice but with a sharper, more ambivalent attitude towards marriage.)

Her predicament can be seen more clearly if you ask yourself whether Belinda will marry one day or is it equally likely that she will live the single life. Is Pope presenting these alternatives in an even-handed manner or does the tone of the poem show that he favours one of them? Must there be loss to achieve gain? There are messages in the theme of change. How you read them depends upon what you believe the poem celebrates, Belinda's virginal beauty or her promise of womanhood.

Does anything in the poem remain stable; does anything last? If the lock survives it does so by the art of Pope's poetry. *The Muse* gives Belinda what physical beauty could not, enduring fame with her name inscribed *midst the stars*. Which of us would remember Arabella Fermor if Pope had not written a poem about her lock? If you consider Pope's decision to be a poet, with all that meant in his personal definition of the role, is it surprising that what began as a light-hearted, private joke intended for a small group of Catholic gentry was extended and polished into a work which places the power of Art above human beauty?

The style of the poem

Structure

When Pope set out to please Caryll by writing something to 'laugh them together again' he chose to write a mock-epic and this decision determined the style of his poem. Even the first version of *The Rape* which lacks many of the epic parallels he was to add later is mock-epic in language and in tone. The five-canto version however follows more closely the structure of the epic.

You may find that you prefer the original version which is printed in Appendix 2. With fewer mock-epic incidents, the narrative line is clearer, the pace quicker and the jokes more obvious to twenty-first-century readers who may lack the background to recognize classical allusions with ease. The greatest change, the introduction of the sylphs, fits so deftly into the five-canto poem that it is astonishing to think they had not been imagined from the start. Could you have told from reading only the five-canto poem which lines were additions? The poem builds to the same climaxes, the public appearance of Belinda, the severing of her lock, the battle for its repossession and the final apotheosis. The additional incidents, the Toilette, the Game of Cards and the Cave of Spleen, allow Pope to expand and deepen the implications of his story. At what cost or gain he does this depends upon your response to the different versions.

Within the poem the structure of the paragraphs creates and reinforces the climaxes. Consider, for example, the closing paragraph of Canto III. The tone is declamatory and epic, set by the grandly (but vaguely) expressed subject, *What Time wou'd spare*, and the reversed syntax of *from Steel receives*. The build-up continues with repetition of phrases and grammatical structures until the paragraph culminates in a mocking deflation of Belinda for imagining that her lock could outlast the towers of Troy. Yet the declamatory tone is held for the resounding final line. Is Belinda enlarged by the mock-epic comparison? Or is she diminished by it?

Clearer examples of how Pope builds his paragraphs towards deflating conclusions are probably Canto I 121–148 and Canto III 1–8. You might like to look at these and consider the effect of their closing couplets. At what point does the tone change from epic to conversational? Is the joke at the end heightened by the build-up which precedes it? Once recognized, you will begin to register further instances of Pope building paragraphs by these methods towards mocking conclusions. Some paragraphs move in the opposite direction. Consider Canto III 147–154 or Canto V 103–112. Starting in the tone of the eighteenth-century drawing-room they end in high epic style. Do the lighter lines make a joke of the concluding couplets or does an echo of the epic lend dignity and pathos to the concluding lines?

Language

Pope uses the standard epic formula of a noun accompanied by an adjective which is elevated and inexact in meaning. A favourite translation of a phrase which occurs repeatedly in the *Iliad* is *wine-dark sea*. Virgil associates his hero with the Latin adjective 'pius' and refers to him constantly as *pius Aeneas*. It is easy to find examples of Pope using this feature of epic style from *dire offense* and *mighty contests* to *verdant fields* and *smoking tyde*.

Pope himself laughed at the familiar formula in *The Art of Sinking* where he called it *periphrase* (which means a round-about way of saying something) or a:

Manner of expressing a known Idea, which should be so misteriously couch'd, as to give the Reader the Pleasure of guessing what it is that the Author can possibly mean: and a Surprise when he finds it.

The Rape is full of phrases where what is intended by the adjective is slightly mysterious: *secret passions, grateful liquors, two-edg'd weapon, fatal shears*. The choice of inflated words and the association of nouns with adjectives grand in tone and vague in meaning are features of the epic and its derivative, the mock-epic. In the mock-epic there is shock as well as surprise when one realizes what the phrase means because the unimportance of the object is highlighted by the grandiose ring of the phrase which describes it. A *two-edg'd weapon* sounds ferocious until one remembers that it is a pair of scissors so tiny that the Baron can hardly fit them on his fingers' ends.

The mock-epic joke lies partly in the imbalance between description and what is being described and partly in sudden, linguistic transitions or bathos (see below) which, without altering the epic formula, juxtapose phrases recalling the high ideals of the epic world, *dire offence, man's imperial race, propitious heav'n, th'imperial tow'rs of Troy*, with phrases which in their colloquial, frivolous, chatty tone belong clearly in the world of the eighteenth century: *elemental Tea, downy pillows, winning lips, midnight masquerades, young Coquettes, bidden blush, giddy circle, tender maid, gentle Damon, tender Billet-doux, burning chocolate, fav'rite Lock*. Epic grandeur is always on the brink of being undercut by the familiar and intimate accents of contemporary gossip.

The heroic couplet: rhythm and rhyme

The Rape is written in the rhythm of the iambic pentameter. Each line has five feet and each foot consists of two syllables, the second of which is stressed. As this amounts to ten syllables in a line, the rhythm is also known as decasyllabic. A rhymed pair of iambic pentameters is called a heroic couplet and this is the style in which Pope wrote *The Rape*.

Pope's rhymes tend on the whole to be monosyllabic: *glade/shade*; *breeze/trees*; *glides/tydes*; *fled/dead*; *found/wound*; *strain/pain*; *must/dust*; *fame/name*. Taken out of context, many have an epic tone. Amidst these expected rhymes Pope slips in ones which lower the tone, mocking and undercutting the epic mode; *mankind/behind*; *bestow/Furbelow*; *brocade/masquerade*; *fail/whale*. These tend to be polysyllabic which creates a lighter tone, but the joke also lies in the oddity of the pairing and the inventiveness of the rhymes. You might like to look at other couplets and consider for yourself the effect of Pope's rhymes.

The same movement of building towards a deflating climax which we saw Pope using in his paragraphs appears in many of the couplets. He often overturns an apparently straightforward meaning by a twist in the couplet's tail. Look, for instance, at the couplet below:

> **While fish in streams, or birds delight in air,**
> **Or in a Coach and six the *British* Fair**   (III 163–164)

The tone of both lines is the same: lightweight, unserious. The first line describes Nature delighting in essential life-giving elements and the second line describes the fashionable set delighting in the show of wealth. The closeness of the comparison is increased by the rhyme which yokes these examples of delight. Yet the juxtaposition is unsettling. There is a qualitative difference between the natural enjoyment of being alive and the self-satisfied enjoyment of luxurious fashion which carries an implicit judgement on the British Fair. Similarly:

> Whether the nymph shall break *Diana's* law,
> Or some frail *China* jar receive a flaw   (II 105–106)

The two disasters are ironically equated and the irony is created by the deceiving nature of the couplet. The two events are closely linked by rhyme and by the couplet's structure which allots them one line apiece, apparently awarding them equal weight. The surprise comes when we realize the accidental nature of the second event and we are left wondering about nymphs who view Diana's law as a matter of accident. Is this a joke or a judgement? The closeness of the comparison is increased by the seemingly parallel phrases *the nymph shall break* and *some frail Chine jar receive* and the subtle difference between them. The first phrase has an active verb and the second a passive one.

Many of the most cutting couplets follow this pattern, an apparently complimentary or neutral first line reversed by the implications of the second line. Statements are called in question by ironic undertones, twists of meaning which surprise by their unexpected wit and acerbity. The reverse can occur in a phrase:

> Now lap-dogs give themselves the rousing shake.
> And sleepless lovers, just at twelve, awake   (I 15–16)

Where the phrase *just at twelve* throws a questioning light on the *sleepless* lovers. It can be created by a single, deftly-placed word. What is the effect of *unfix'd* in the following couplet?

> Her lively looks a sprightly mind disclose,
> Quick as her eyes, and as unfix'd as those   (II 9–10)

There are many other moments in the poem where you will recognize Pope turning the couplet to his satiric purposes. Perhaps the deflation is nowhere more apparent than in the *double-entendres*. Consider the implications of the closing of the couplets IV 175–176, V 77–78 and V 97–98.

The iambic pentameter and the closing of each couplet with a rhyme mean that Pope is writing in a highly restrictive mode. The formal restraints of his chosen style mirror the world of artifice and decorum which his poem describes. Like the china jar, the flowered brocade and the trembling sylphs, his couplets are held in a delicate state of poise and tension which cannot be broken without damage. In passion and anger, Belinda and the Baron may overstep the bounds, but Pope's couplets never falter. In this assured control lies much of the wit and charm of the poem.

Poetic devices

Pope uses various established and recognized poetic methods of writing in a comical and belittling manner.

Bathos: a sudden shift of tone which produces a comical effect by means of an unexpected descent from exalted content and language to the banal and ordinary. For example, in the line stating that great Anna, *Dost sometimes counsel take – and sometimes Tea* (III 8) content moves from important State business, *counsel*, to simple behaviour, taking *Tea*, so rapidly that the effect is startlingly and amusingly discordant. In the couplet *Not tyrants fierce that unrepenting die,/Not Cynthia when her manteau's pinn'd awry*, (IV 7–8) the high epic language of the first line contrasts bathetically with the mundane vocabulary of the second. (You might like to consider whether the contrasts in the preceding two couplets are a bathetic descent, or a satiric joke against ageing women.) Bathos is a diminishing comic device which Pope uses throughout the poem to poke fun at his characters' inflated sense of their own importance, yet he uses it ambiguously.

Zeugma: the technical term given to a device Pope uses frequently in *The Rape*. A single verb governs two objects and is used in a different sense in each case, for example, in the lines quoted above, that *great* ANNA... *Dost sometimes counsel take – and sometimes Tea* (III 8) where advice and a cup of tea are both proper objects of the verb 'to take' but read incongruously when used at the same time. Or in the description of Sir Plume who *first the snuff-box open'd, then the case* (IV 126), where again it is grammatically correct to open both a snuff-box and a legal case but it sounds oddly awry when the phrases are set so closely together. One effect of this device is to add to the humorous atmosphere of the poem. There is a quirkiness which puzzles and delights as we sense the solution almost at the moment of hesitant misunderstanding.

In other ways, however, Pope's use of zeugma seems to go to the heart of his mocking and ambiguous attitude towards Belinda and reflects his judgement of her world. There is a sense that, if not to the reader then at least to ANNA and Sir Plume, the incongruously different objects are of equal importance. If Queen Anne takes counsel in the spirit in which she drinks tea, what does this imply about the seriousness with which she treats state business?

Activity

Think about the effect of Pope's use of zeugma in these lines:

Or stain her honour, or her new brocade,	(II 107)
Or lose her heart, or necklace, at a ball;	(II 109)

Discussion

What strikes me first is the unexpectedness of the things lost and stained, or rather the amusing unexpectedness of their conjunction. Is Ariel not right to feel that any of these mishaps would be upsetting? And yet it seems ridiculous to equate them as the grammar and the satisfying sound of the neatly balanced lines suggests. If one searches for the sense of disturbance where it appears to lie, in the meaning of the lines, is Pope's attitude any clearer? Are we to take the juxtaposition as a joke; as an ironic comment upon the moral disorder of the poem's characters; as a judgement on a world which values fashion and entertainment as the business of life? Or are we to see it as a sympathetic response to virginal belles whose beauty is as precious and as delicate as a china jar and whose sexual attractiveness requires both exposure and protection? You may have found another reading of these elusive lines. The ambiguity of zeugma opens up multiple possibilities.

Irony: the humorous or mildly sarcastic use of words to imply the opposite of what, on the surface, is intended. The Baron's apparent compliment to Sir Plume as someone *Who speaks so well*, (IV 132) is ironic, since it is clear that Sir Plume's stumbling request to return the curl is the opposite of speaking *well*. You might like to consider the meanings, overt and implied, of *strange* (I 7), *three garters* (II 39), *maladies* (IV 37), *no more* (V 78), and to look yourself for further instances of Pope's undercutting of surface meaning with subtly judgemental irony.

Satire: a literary form dating from the classical period in which events and issues, usually contemporary and often political, are attacked by being held up to witty ridicule. Dr Johnson defined satire as 'a poem in which wickedness or folly is censured'. In 1726 Pope's friend, Jonathan Swift published *Gulliver's Travels* as a satire on the trial of the impeached Tory leader, Robert Harley and in 1729, *A Modest Proposal* which satirized the state of poverty in Ireland. Another friend John Gay wrote *The Beggars' Opera* in 1728 as a satiric condemnation of corrupt government. Later in his life, Pope also wrote satires attacking the governing Whig party and their leader, Robert Walpole but he would not himself have called *The Rape* a satire because to him the comic elements of exaggeration, bathos and irony are part of the mock-heroic, a gentler form of mockery which contrasts high epic ideals with less heroic contemporary life. It is however a term commonly applied by later critics to the way in which *The Rape* ridicules and belittles the fashionable world of beaux and belles obsessed with *trivial things*. David Fairer 1989, for example, writes 'The word "trivial" is frequently used by critics about the poem. Those who dislike it find it trivial in itself; some who admire it see it as a satire on triviality.'

Imagery

The fragility of precious objects as an image of Belinda's beauty, sexuality and honour has been discussed. I want now to look more closely at other image patterns in the poem. The first is formed by the noun clusters, the lists of oddly random, assorted things; the confusion and profusion on Belinda's dressing table; the things lost on earth and treasured in the lunar sphere; Thalestris' list of beauty aids; unnumbered things in the Cave of Spleen; the Baron's love offerings. They share the quality of being jackdaw collections. They seem to operate as a symbol of the arbitrary possessiveness of the material world of beaux and belles who cannot distinguish between virginity and vases, necklaces and hearts, lovers and lapdogs, between honour as outward show and honour as an ideal form of behaviour.

The sun is probably the clearest example of a symbol which pervades the poem and helps to carry its themes. Throughout, the reader knows that the claim that Belinda rivals or eclipses the sun must be false and that knowledge is one of the jokes against her. Recognition of the transience of Belinda's beauty lies at the heart of Pope's teasing symbol of the sun. The poem closes with the reality that *those fair suns*, her eyes, *must set*. Even as one light is dimmed, another rises. There always was a sphere in which things were rightly valued. The lock takes its place in the *heav'ns*, above the lower world of the *Lunar sphere*. Sun and star represent the firm, sure, eternal world which lies beyond the lower world of Belinda and the sylphs.

Critical history

The Rape of the Lock was an immediate success, a best seller in 1714. The only complaints came from Pope's enemies for whom Belinda's behaviour, particularly her *double entendres*, was an easy target: a lady must not be vulgar, either in deportment or speech. 'You must make the Ladies speak Bawdy, no matter whether they are Women of honour or not... . Thus a Friend of mine has lately, with admirable Address, made Arabella F _ m _ r prefer the Lock of her Poll, to her Locks of another more sacred and secret Part', (Gildon, *Evening Post*, 1714). Dennis ('Remarks on Mr Pope's Rape of the Lock', 1728) criticized the poem as 'a very empty Trifle' and he too castigated 'the Manners and Behaviour of his (Pope's) fine Lady, who is so very rampant, and so very a Termagant'. However, Dennis published these remarks, 'with very little force, and with no effect, for the opinion of the public was already settled', wrote Dr Johnson who summed up the general opinion of eighteenth-century critics when he described the poem as 'the most exquisite example of ludicrous poetry'.

Addison called the 1712 version a 'delicious little thing' but when Pope asked him about enlarging it, he replied that it needed no additions. Apparently a compliment, his comment contains the kernel of a dismissal which undervalued the poem in the nineteenth century. 'There is no finer gem than this poem in all the lighter treasures of English fancy' (Campbell, *Edinburgh Review*, 1808). 'That exquisite little toilette-bottle of essence' (Leigh Hunt 1817). 'It is the most exquisite specimen of fillagree work ever invented... It is made of gauze and silver spangles. The most glittering appearance is given to every thing, to paste, pomatum, billet-doux, and patches. Airs, languid airs, breathe around: – the atmosphere is perfumed with affectation... The little is made great, and the great little. You hardly know whether to laugh or to weep. It is the triumph of insignificance, the apotheosis of foppery and folly' (Hazlitt, *On Dryden and Pope*, 1818). Alongside praise runs the sense that the poem is a *little thing*, a masterpiece diminished by its trivial subject. Do you agree?

Pope's physical disability was commented upon, both as an inspiration for and a limitation on his writings. 'Great natural advantages are seldom combined with great acquired ones... If Pope had been a beautiful youth, he would not have written *The Rape of the Lock*', wrote Hazlitt and, less kindly, Leigh Hunt (*Wit and Humour*, 1846): 'The little fragile creature had wings; and he could expand them at will, and ascend, if to no great imaginative height, yet to charming fairy circles just above those of the world about him, disclosing enchanting visions at the top of drawing rooms, and enabling us to see the spirits that wait on coffee-cups and hoop petticoats'.

In the early twentieth century critics began to reject diminishing terms such as *fillagree* and *foppery*. Tillotson (1938) claimed: 'Because a poem is about the work of a pair of scissors on a lock of hair, it is not therefore necessarily a trivial poem'. It became considered irrelevant to refer to the personal circumstances of an author in any discussion of the works. Literature was studied as a linguistic mode in which genre dictated the choice of vocabulary. A poem, like a novel, was held to be an artefact made of words, with all the connotations words carry. Writing was separated from the writer: texts explored in isolation. This emphasis on close analysis highlighted Pope's craftsmanship: the care he took over the choice of individual words, his attention to the rules of genre, his classical allusions, the deliberate borrowings from older poets, his use of images and symbols, the variety of his rhymes and rhythms. Studying the formal qualities of *The Rape* led to a greater appreciation of the poem's depth and subtlety.

Since the marxist-materialist, feminist and new historicist approaches of the mid-to-late-twentieth century, critics no longer feel comfortable divorcing a text from the period in which it was created, but the rewards of close analysis remain. It is always revealing to look closely at Pope's technical achievements and ask yourself how they influence the way you respond to the poem.

Materialist critics in the mid-twentieth-century related the poem to the historical circumstances of its production and reception. Foregrounding England's trading successes, they read Belinda as a precious object, an ornament which has market value. 'Belinda's presentation of herself as an object originates in her society's reduction of all value to money value, all life to commodity... . The right use of beauty is not to tease a man, but to catch a man: a husband is "what beauty gains"' (Delany 1975).

'If Belinda stands for the products of mercantilism, her story in turn enacts the violence of imperial war. Battles dominate Cantos III and V; and war pervades the poem' (Brown 1985).

Feminist theory linked ideas about women as commodities to their unequal position in eighteenth-century society, arguing that 'women's entire value is tied up with her identity as a piece of property transferable among men' (Pollak 1985). In this reading, Belinda's autonomy depends upon her remaining single while at the same time she derives her power from her attractiveness in the sexual stakes, a value conferred by male admiration. The poem is 'persistently collapsing Belinda's subjectivity into her status as an object, and specifically as an object of male desire and ownership. Manifestly, Belinda is at the centre of Pope's fictional universe, as she is – as the belle of the ball – at the centre of Hampton Court society where all eyes are fixed on her alone (II 6). Dramatically speaking, the Baron seems to play a relatively insignificant role. As a presence in the poem he almost seems a kind of shadow of Belinda; he doesn't even have a proper name. Ideologically, however, it is Belinda who is situated on the margins of the text' (Pollak 1985).

Late-twentieth-century scholars investigating the book trade recognized how carefully Pope had supervised the publication of the second, expensive version of *The Rape*. Laverty (2001) observed: 'He loved the look of print: dropped heads, italics, black letter, caps, and smalls; fine paper, wide margins, and good ink; headpieces, tailpieces, initials, and plates.' The visual appearance of a text is part of its meaning. Pope insisted upon illustrations and decorations. Consider how the layout and illustrations in this edition affect your reading of *The Rape*. Would you have preferred the spacious layout of Pope's first edition of the poem which took forty-eight pages and allowed no more than twenty lines per page?

Recent scholarship has looked more carefully at the circle of Catholic friends and acquaintances to whom the poem was first addressed and at the insecurity of their lives after the Glorious Revolution. Marriage, while not a certainty, (neither Arabella nor

Lord Petre were married when Pope first wrote *The Rape*) was the expected goal of a young woman, her duty, her role in the landed gentry and aristocratic society to which the original recipients belonged. Social stability and dynastic marriage required a degree of self-control over instinct and passion which the rules of good manners aimed to provide. 'In Pope's poem, sexual rapaciousness is sublimated into a courtship ritual. The card-game also is a mating dance and a ritualised expression of potentially violent sexual energy'(Weinbrot 1988). In this reading Clarissa's advice is a moral argument for obligation. Whereas feminist criticism saw Belinda losing power if she abandoned her single state, the emphasis on social obligation sees in marriage 'not the death of the individual but the continuity of the group' (Weinbrot 1997). If Belinda is being urged, however jokingly, towards marriage then the poem can be read as a lesson in the importance of good manners and the value of politeness, the final polish which transforms a beautiful and spirited young lady into a saintly wife. On the occasion of her marriage, Pope wrote to Arabella, echoing words from the poem.

> You are by this time satisfy'd how much the tenderness of one man of merit is to be prefer'd to the addresses of a thousand... It was but just, that the same Virtues which gave you reputation, should give you happiness; and I can wish you no greater, than that you may receive it in as high a degree your self, as so much good humour must infallibly give it to your husband.
>
> It may be expected perhaps, that one who has the title of Poet, should say something more polite on this occasion: But I am really more a well-wisher to your felicity, than a celebrator of your beauty. Besides, you are now a married woman, and in a way to be a great many better things than a fine Lady; such as an excellent wife, a faithful friend, a tender parent, and at last as the consequence of them all, a saint in heaven.

Belinda, however, neither loses nor keeps her lock. What implications does this have for Pope's attitude towards women? Do you feel the poem celebrates the autonomy of independence, youth and beauty or the importance of restraint, good manners and obligation? Is the subject *an empty trifle*? Indeed, what is the subject – Belinda, the lock, marriage, manners, Pope's own poetry, or an amusing *jest*?

Essay Questions

1 'Beauty draws us with a single hair.' Identify the ways in which Pope creates a sense of Belinda's beauty for the reader and discuss the complexity of his attitude towards her.

2 In the final analysis do you find the poem's presentation of Belinda mocking or sympathetic?

3 'She has got herself up to hunt, to prey, to capture.' 'Belinda is the innocent victim of a rude assault.' How far do you agree with both of these views?

4 What do Thalestris and Clarissa contribute to the poem?

5 Thalestris refers to Belinda's lock as *th'inestimable prize*. How does Pope create a sense of the lock's value and why do you think it is so prized?

6 Clarissa has been called both wise and worldly wise. Is it possible to agree with both judgements?

7 Starting with Thalestris' speech, Canto IV 95–120, consider what evidence there is in the poem of difficulties faced by women, even wealthy ones, in the eighteenth century.

8 What picture of an of eighteenth-century gentleman do you receive from Pope's presentation of the Baron?

9 The Baron has been called both aggressor and victim. What evidence is there in the poem to support both of these views?

10 The fashionable world of *The Rape* has been described positively: 'the most glittering appearance is given to everything' and negatively: 'Pope never allows us to forget that it is a world whose ethical judgements are in sad disarray.' How far can both of these judgements be justified by the text of the poem?

11 The sylphs have been described as symbolizing 'the triviality of Belinda's world'. To what extent do you agree with this statement?

12 'Hearts and necklaces, lap-dogs and lovers, statesmanship and tea, queens and Indian screens, the hunger of jurymen and justice, Bibles and billet-doux: the verse of the poem entangles these trifles and values together in order to reflect a similar entanglement in this society's mind.' To what extent do you agree with this statement?

14 What do you feel you have learned about life in eighteenth-century London from reading *The Rape*?

15 Remind yourself of the section Canto I 121–148. How would you defend the view that this section is the key to the whole poem?

16 Re-read the final section of the poem, Canto V 123–150. Do you find this a fitting climax to the poem or do you feel that Pope is failing to offer solutions to the issues raised in the text? Is it possible to agree with both opinions?

17 *The Rape* is written in the genre of mock-epic. Illustrate Pope's use of the mock-heroic style with examples taken from the poem as a whole. Do you find this style amusing or over-elaborate?

18 Choose a section of about 20 lines which appeals to you and show how Pope's use of paragraph, couplet, vocabulary, tone, rhythm, rhyme and poetic devices contribute to the effect of the passage.

19 Select examples of what you consider to be inappropriate as well as appropriate uses of the heroic idiom. In each case, explain and discuss your choice.

20 The purpose of the poem was to laugh two quarrelling families together again. Drawing on the whole text, show how Pope satirizes the cutting-off of a lock of hair. To what extent do you feel he succeeds in making a jest of the incident?

21 Illustrate the comic ways in which Pope magnifies the importance of trivialities. Do you feel his methods prevent the reader from taking anything in the poem seriously?

22 Pope has been accused of being both critical and admiring of the rich, idle life he portrays in the poem. Try to provide evidence to justify both approaches.

23 Pope described the subject of the poem as 'the life of modern ladies in this idle Town'. To what extent would you accept his description and to what extent would you wish to argue that the poem has other concerns?

24 Discuss the handling of the themes of time and change in the poem.

Chronology

Events in Pope's life

Historical events

Year	Historical events
1679–81	The Exclusion crisis. The Whig party make several attempts to pass a bill in Parliament excluding the Roman Catholic James, Duke of York, from the succession.
1685	Death of Charles II and accession of James II.
1688	Flight of James II to France. William of Orange lands in England.
1689	Accession of William and Mary.
1701	The Act of Settlement provides for a Protestant heir to the English throne. The Pretender is recognized by Louis XIV. England at war with France.
1702	Death of William and accession of Anne.
1704	Marlborough defeats the French at the Battle of Blenheim.
1707	Union of England and Scotland.

Year	Events in Pope's life
1688	Pope born in London.
1700	Pope's family move from London to Binfield perhaps to escape the ten-mile law against Catholics.
1705	Pope begins to visit London and meet with literary men.
1709	Pope's early poems published in Tonson's *Miscellanies*.

Year	Literary events	Year	Historical events
1711	Pope's *Essay on Criticism* published.	1713	Peace treaty concluded with France.
1712	*The Rape of the Locke* published.	1714	Death of Anne and accession of George I.
1714	The enlarged version of *The Rape of the Lock* published.	1715	Jacobite rebellion.
1715	Pope starts publishing his translation of the *Iliad*.		
1717	Clarissa's speech added to *The Rape of the Lock*.		
1718	Pope and his mother move to Twickenham.		
		1720	South Sea Bubble scandal.
		1721	Walpole becomes Lord Treasurer.
		1727	Death of George I and accession of George II.
1728	Pope's *Dunciad* published.		
1731	*Moral Essay IV* published.		
1733	*Moral Essay III* published.		
1734	*Moral Essay I* and *Essay on Man* published.		
1735	*Epistle to Arbuthnot* and *Moral Essay II* published.		
1743	*The Dunciad* published (with an additional book).	1739	England at war with Spain.
1744	Pope dies.		
		1745	Jacobite rebellion.

Further Reading

Editions

Geoffrey Tillotson (ed.), *The Rape of the Lock and Other Poems* (Methuen, 1940)

Clarence Tracy (ed.), *The Rape Observ'd* (University of Toronto Press, 1974)

Cynthia Wall (ed.), *The Rape of the Lock* (Macmillan, 1998)

Biography

Maynard Mack, *Alexander Pope: A Life* (Yale University Press, 1985)

Netta Murray Goldsmith, *Alexander Pope: The Evolution of a Poet* (Ashgate, 2002)

Critical books

Reuben A. Brower, *Alexander Pope: The Poetry of Allusion* (Oxford, 1959)

Laura Brown, *Alexander Pope* (Basil Blackwell, 1985)

David Fairer, *The Poetry of Alexander Pope* (Penguin Critical Studies, 1989)

John A. Jones, *Pope's Couplet Art* (Ohio University Press, 1969)

James McLaverty, *Pope, Print and Meaning* (Oxford, 2001)

Ellen Pollak, *The Poetics of Sexual Myth* (University of Chicago Press, 1985)

Pat Rogers, *Pope and the Destiny of the Stuarts* (Oxford, 2005)

Thomas Woodman, *Politeness and Poetry in the Age of Pope* (Associated University Presses, 1989)

Collections of articles

Brean Hammond (ed.), *Pope* (Longman, 1996)

John Dixon Hunt (ed.), *The Rape of the Lock: A Casebook* (Macmillan, 1968)

Maynard Mack (ed.), *Essential Articles for the Study of Alexander Pope* (Archon, 1968)

Maynard Mack (ed.), *Pope: Recent Essays by Several Hands* (Archon, 1980)

G.S. Rousseau (ed.), *Twentieth-Century Interpretations of The Rape of the Lock* (Prentice-Hall, 1969)

Additional articles

Sheila Delany, 'Sex and Politics in Pope's *Rape of the Lock*', *English Studies in Canada*, 1975

Hugh Kenner, 'Pope's Reasonable Rhymes', *English Literary History 41*, 1974

Louis Landa, 'Pope's Belinda, The General Emporie of the World, and the Wondrous Worm', *Essays in Eighteenth-Century English Literature* (Princeton University Press, 1980)

Howard D. Weinbrot, 'The Rape of the Lock and the Contexts of Warfare', *Eighteenth-Century Satire* (Cambridge University Press, 1988)

Howard D. Weinbrot, 'Fine, Ladies, Saints in Heaven, and Pope's *Rape of the Lock*', *Augustan Studies* (Associated University Presses, 1997)

Appendix 1

Before Pope published his second, fuller version of the poem in 1714 he offered two alternative introductions to Arabella Fermor for her approval. She chose the prose dedication which has traditionally accompanied the poem ever since. This little poem was published anonymously in 1717 in a miscellany which Pope edited and later editors of his works believe that it is the discarded introduction to *The Rape of the Lock*.

To BELINDA on *THE RAPE OF THE LOCK*

> Pleas'd in these lines, *Belinda*, you may view
> How things are priz'd, which once belong'd to you.
> If on some meaner head this Lock had grown,
> The nymph despis'd, the Rape had been unknown.
> 5 But what concerns the valiant and the fair,
> The Muse asserts as her peculiar care.
> Thus *Helens* Rape and *Menelaus'* wrong
> Became the Subject of great *Homer's* song;
> And, lost in ancient times, the golden fleece
> 10 Was rais'd to fame by all the wits of *Greece*.
>
>   Had fate decreed, propitious to your pray'rs,
> To give their utmost date to all your hairs;
> This Lock, of which late ages now shall tell,
> Had dropt like fruit, neglected, when it fell.
>
> 15 Nature to your undoing arms mankind
> With strength of body, artifice of mind;
> But gives your feeble sex, made up of fears,
> No guard but virtue, no redress but tears.
> Yet custom (seldom to your favour gain'd)
> 20 Absolves the virgin when by force constrain'd
> Thus *Lucrece* lives unblemish'd in her fame,

A bright example of young *Tarquin's* shame.
Such praise is yours – and such shall you possess.
Your virtue equal, tho' your loss be less.
25 Then smile Belinda at reproachful tongues,
Still warm our hearts, and still inspire our songs.
But would your charms to distant times extend,
Let *Jervas* paint them, and let *Pope* commend.
Who censure most, more precious hairs would lose,
30 To have the *Rape* recorded by his Muse.

Appendix 2

The first version of the poem, published in 1712.

THE RAPE of the LOCKE
An Heroi-comical POEM

> *Nolueram*, Belinda, *tuos violare capillos,*
> *Sed juvat hoc precibus me tribuisse tuis.*
> MART. Lib. 12. Ep. 86.

Canto I

What dire Offence from Am'rous causes springs,
What mighty Quarrels rise from Trivial Things,
I sing – this verse to C——l, Muse! is due;
This, ev'n *Belinda* may vouchsafe to view;
5   Slight is the subject, but not so the Praise,
If She inspire, and He approve my Lays.

    Say what strange Motive, Goddess! cou'd compel
A well-bred *Lord* t'assault a gentle *Belle?*
Oh say what stranger Cause, yet unexplor'd,
10   Cou'd make a gentle *Belle* reject a *Lord?*
And dwells such Rage in *softest Bosoms* then?
And lodge such daring Souls in *Little Men?*

    Sol thro' white Curtains did his Beams display,
And op'd those Eyes which brighter shine than they;
15   *Shock* just had giv'n himself the rowzing Shake,
And Nymphs prepar'd their *Chocolate* to take;
Thrice the wrought Slipper knock'd against the Ground,
And striking Watches the tenth Hour resound.
Belinda rose, and 'midst attending Dames

20   Launch'd on the Bosom of the silver *Thames*:
     A Train of well-drest Youths around her shone,
     And ev'ry Eye was fix'd on her alone.
     On her white Breast a sparkling *Cross* she wore,
     Which *Jews* might kiss, and Infidels adore.
25   Her lively Looks a sprightly Mind disclose,
     Quick as her Eyes, and as unfixt as those:
     Favours to none, to all she Smiles extends;
     Oft she rejects, but never once offends.
     Bright as the Sun her Eyes the Gazers strike,
30   And, like the Sun, they shine on all alike.
     Yet graceful Ease, and Sweetness void of Pride,
     Might hide her Faults, if *Belles* had Faults to hide:
     If to her share some Female Errors fall,
     Look on her Face, and you'll forgive 'em all.

35   This Nymph, to the Destruction of Mankind,
     Nourish'd two Locks, which graceful hung behind
     In equal Curls, and well conspir'd to deck
     With shining Ringlets the smooth Iv'ry Neck.
     Love in these Labyrinths his Slaves detains,
40   And mighty Hearts are held in slender Chains.
     With hairy Sprindges we the Birds betray,
     Slight Lines of Hair surprize the Finny Prey,
     Fair Tresses Man's Imperial Race insnare,
     And Beauty draws us with a *single Hair*.

45   Th'Advent'rous *Baron* the bright Locks admir'd,
     He saw, he wish'd, and to the Prize aspir'd:
     Resolv'd to win, he meditates the way,
     By Force to ravish, or by Fraud betray;
     For when Success a Lover's Toil attends,
50   Few ask, if Fraud or Force attain'd his Ends.
     For this, ere *Phœbus* rose, he had implor'd
     Propitious Heav'n, and ev'ry Pow'r ador'd,
     But chiefly *Love* – to *Love* an Altar built,

Of twelve vast *French* Romances, neatly gilt.
55 There lay the Sword-knot *Sylvia's* Hands had sown,
With *Flavia's* Busk that oft had rapp'd his own:
A fan, a Garter, half a Pair of Gloves;
And all the Trophies of his former Loves.
With tender *Billet-doux* he lights the Pyre,
60 And breathes three am'rous Sighs to raise the Fire,
Then prostrate falls, and begs with ardent Eyes
Soon to obtain, and long possess the Prize:
The Pow'rs gave Ear, and granted half his Pray'r,
The rest, the Winds dispers'd in empty Air.

65 Close by those Meads for ever crown'd with Flow'rs,
Where *Thames* with Pride surveys his rising Tow'rs,
There stands a Structure of Majestick Frame,
Which from the neighb'ring *Hampton* takes its Name.
Here *Britain's* Statesmen oft the Fall foredoom
70 Of foreign Tyrants, and of Nymphs at home;
Here Thou, great *Anna!* whom three Realms obey,
Dost sometimes Counsel take – and sometimes *Tea*.

Hither our Nymphs and Heroes did resort,
To taste awhile the Pleasures of a Court;
75 In various Talk the chearful hours they past,
Of, who was *Bitt*, or who *Capotted* last:
This speaks the glory of the *British Queen*,
And that describes a charming *Indian Screen*;
A third interprets Motions, Looks, and Eyes;
80 At ev'ry Word a Reputation dies.
Snuff, or the *Fan*, supply each Pause of Chatt,
With singing, laughing, ogling, and all that.
Now, when declining from the Noon of Day,
The Sun obliquely shoots his burning Ray;
85 When hungry Judges soon the Sentence sign,
And Wretches hang that Jury-men may Dine;
When Merchants from th'*Exchange* return in Peace,

And the long Labours of the *Toilette* cease –
The Board's with Cups and Spoons, alternate, crown'd;
90   The Berries crackle, and the mill turns round;
On shining Altars of *Japan* they raise
The silver *Lamp*; the fiery Spirits blaze;
From silver Spouts the grateful Liquors glide,
And *China's* earth receives the smoking Tyde:
95   At once they gratifie their Smell and Taste,
While frequent Cups prolong the rich Repast.
Coffee, (which makes the Politician wise,
And see thro' all things with his half-shut Eyes)
Sent up in Vapours to the *Baron's* Brain
100   New Stratagems, the radiant Locke to gain.
Ah cease, rash Youth! desist e'er 'tis too late,
Fear the just Gods, and think of *Scylla's* Fate!
Chang'd to a bird, and sent to flitt in Air,
She dearly pays for *Nisus'* injur'd Hair!

105   But when to Mischief Mortals bend their Mind,
How soon fit Instruments of Ill they find?
Just then, *Clarissa* drew with tempting Grace
A two-edg'd Weapon from her shining Case;
So Ladies in Romance assist their Knight,
110   Present the Spear, and arm him for the Fight.
He takes the Gift with rev'rence, and extends
The little Engine on his Finger's Ends,
This just behind *Belinda's* Neck he spread,
As o'er the fragrant Steams she bends her Head:
115   He first expands the glitt'ring *Forfex* wide
T'inclose the Lock; then joins it, to divide;
One fatal stroke the sacred Hair does sever
From the fair Head, for ever, and for ever!

The living Fires come flashing from her Eyes,
120   And Screams of Horror rend th'affrighted Skies.
Not louder Shrieks by Dames to Heav'n are cast,

When Husbands die, or *Lap-dogs* breath their last,
Or when rich *China* Vessels fal'n from high,
In glitt'ring Dust and painted Fragments lie!

125   Let Wreaths of triumph now my Temples twine,
(The Victor cry'd) the glorious Prize is mine!
While Fish in Streams, or Birds delight in Air,
Or in a Coach and Six the *British* Fair,
As long as *Atalantis* shall be read,
130   Or the small Pillow grace a Lady's Bed,
While *Visits* shall be paid on solemn Days,
When num'rous Wax-lights in bright Order blaze,
While Nymphs take Treats, or Assignations give,
So long my Honour, Name, and Praise shall live!

135   What Time wou'd spare, from Steel receives its date,
And Monuments, like Men, submit to Fate!
Steel did the labour of the Gods destroy,
And strike to Dust th'aspiring Tow'rs of *Troy*;
Steel cou'd the works of mortal Pride confound,
140   And hew Triumphal Arches to the ground.
What Wonder then, fair Nymph! thy Hairs shou'd feel
The conqu'ring Force of unresisted Steel?

Canto II

But anxious Cares the pensive Nymph opprest,
And secret Passions labour'd in her Breast.
Not youthful Kings in Battle seiz'd alive,
Not scornful Virgins who their Charms survive,
5   Not ardent Lover robb'd of all his Bliss,
Not ancient Lady when refus'd a Kiss,
Not Tyrants fierce that unrepenting die,
Not *Cynthia* when her *Manteau's* pinn'd awry,

E'er felt such Rage, Resentment, and Despair,
10   As Thou, sad Virgin! for thy ravish'd Hair.

    While her rackt Soul Repose and Peace requires,
  The fierce *Thalestris* fans the rising Fires.
  O wretched Maid (she spread her hands, and cry'd,
  And *Hampton's* Ecchoes, wretched Maid! reply'd)
15   Was it for this you took such constant Care,
  Combs, Bodkins, Leads, Pomatums, to prepare?
  For this your Locks in Paper Durance bound,
  For this with tort'ring Irons wreath'd around?
  Oh had the Youth but been content to seize
20   Hairs less in sight – or any Hairs but these!
  Gods! shall the Ravisher display this Hair,
  While the Fops envy, and the Ladies stare!
  Honour forbid! at whose unrival'd Shrine
  Ease, Pleasure, Virtue, All, our Sex resign.
25   Methinks already I your Tears survey,
  Already hear the horrid things they say,
  Already see you a degraded Toast,
  And all your Honour in a Whisper lost!
  How shall I, then, your helpless Fame defend?
30   'Twill then be Infamy to seem your Friend!
  And shall this Prize, th' inestimable Prize,
  Expos'd thro' *Crystal* to the gazing Eyes,
  And heightened by the *Diamond's* circling Rays,
  On that Rapacious Hand for ever blaze?
35   Sooner shall grass in *Hide-Park Circus* grow,
  And Wits take Lodgings in the Sound of *Bow*;
  Sooner let Earth, Air, Sea, to *Chaos* fall,
  Men, Monkies, Lap-dogs, Parrots, perish all!

    She said; then raging to *Sir Plume* repairs,
40   And bids her *Beau* demand the precious Hairs:
  (*Sir Plume*, of *Amber Snuff-box* justly vain,
  And the nice Conduct of a *clouded Cane*)

With earnest Eyes, and round unthinking Face,
He first the Snuff-box open'd, then the Case,
45 And thus broke out – 'My Lord, why, what the Devil?
'Z——ds! damn the Lock! 'fore Gad, you must be civil
'Plague on't! 'tis past a Jest – nay prithee, Pox!
'Give her the Hair' – he spoke, and rapp'd his Box.

It grieves me much (reply'd the Peer again)
50 Who speaks so well shou'd ever speak in vain.
But by this Locke, this sacred Locke I swear,
(Which never more shall join its parted Hair,
Which never more its Honours shall renew,
Clip'd from the lovely Head where once it grew)
55 That while my Nostrils draw the vital Air,
This Hand, which won it, shall for ever wear.
He spoke, and speaking, in proud Triumph spread
The long-contended Honours of her Head.

But see! the *Nymph* in Sorrow's Pomp appears,
60 Her Eyes half-languishing, half-drown'd in Tears;
Now livid pale her Cheeks, now glowing red;
On her heav'd Bosom hung her drooping Head,
Which, with a Sigh, she rais'd; and thus she said.

For ever curs'd be this detested Day,
65 Which snatch'd my best, my fav'rite Curl away!
Happy! ah ten times happy, had I been,
If *Hampton-Court* these Eyes had never seen!
Yet am not I the first mistaken Maid,
By Love of Courts to num'rous Ills betray'd.
70 Oh had I rather un-admir'd remain'd
In some lone *Isle*, or distant *Northern* Land;
Where the gilt *Chariot* never mark'd the way,
Where none learn *Ombre*, none e'er taste *Bohea*!
There kept my Charms conceal'd from mortal Eye,
75 Like Roses, that in Desarts bloom and die.

What mov'd my Mind with youthful Lords to rome?
O had I stay'd, and said my Pray'rs at home!
'Twas this, the Morning *Omens* did foretel;
Thrice from my trembling hand the *Patch-box* fell;
80   The tott'ring *China* shook without a Wind,
Nay, *Poll* sat, mute, and *Shock* was most *Unkind!*
See the poor Remnants of this slighted Hair!
My hands shall rend what ev'n thy own did spare.
This, in two sable Ringlets taught to break,
85   Once gave new Beauties to the snowie Neck;
The Sister-Locke now sits uncouth, alone,
And in its Fellow's Fate foresees its own;
Uncurl'd it hangs! the fatal Sheers demands;
And tempts once more thy sacrilegious Hands.

90   She said: the pitying Audience melt in Tears,
But *Fate* and *Jove* had stopp'd the *Baron's* ears.
In vain *Thalestris* with Reproach assails,
For who can move when fair *Belinda* fails?
Not half so fix'd the *Trojan* cou'd remain,
95   While *Anna* begg'd and *Dido* rag'd in vain.
To Arms, to Arms! the bold *Thalestris* cries,
And swift as Lightning to the Combate flies.
All side in Parties, and begin th'Attack;
Fans clap, Silks russle and tough whalebones crack;
100   Heroes and Heroins Shouts confus'dly rise,
And base, and treble Voices strike the Skies.
No common Weapons in their Hands are found,
Like Gods they fight, nor dread a mortal Wound.

So when bold *Homer* makes the Gods engage,
105   And heav'nly Breasts with human Passions rage;
'Gainst *Pallas*, *Mars*; *Latona*, *Hermes* Arms;
And all *Olympus* rings with loud Alarms.
Jove's Thunder roars, Heav'n trembles all around;
Blue *Neptune* storms, the bellowing Deeps resound;

110   *Earth* shakes her nodding Tow'rs, the Ground gives way,
And the pale Ghosts start at the Flash of Day!

While thro' the Press enrag'd *Thalestris* flies,
And scatters Deaths around from both her Eyes,
A *Beau* and *Witling* perish'd in the Throng,
115   One dy'd in *Metaphor*, and one in *Song*.
O cruel Nymph! a living Death I bear
Cry'd *Dapperwit*, and sunk beside his Chair.
A mournful Glance Sir *Fopling* upwards cast,
Those eyes are made so killing – was his last:
120   Thus on *Meander's* flow'ry Margin lies
Th' expiring Swan, and as he sings he dies.

As bold Sir *Plume* had drawn *Clarissa* down,
Chloë stept in, and kill'd him with a Frown;
She smil'd to see the doughty Hero slain,
125   But at her Smile, the Beau reviv'd again.

Now *Jove* suspends his golden Scales in Air,
Weighs the Mens Wits against the Lady's Hair;
The doubtful Beam long nods from side to side;
At length the Wits mount up, the Hairs subside.

130   See Fierce *Belinda* on the *Baron* flies,
With more than usual Lightning in her Eyes;
Nor fear'd the Chief th'unequal Fight to try,
Who sought no more than on his Foe to die.
But this bold Lord, with manly Strength indu'd,
135   She with one Finger and a Thumb subdu'd:
Just where the breath of Life his Nostrils drew,
A Charge of *Snuff* the wily Virgin threw;
Sudden, with starting Tears each Eye o'erflows,
And the high Dome re-ecchoes to his Nose.

140   Now meet thy Fate, th'incens'd Virago cry'd,
And drew a deadly *Bodkin* from her Side.
Boast not my Fall (he said) insulting Foe!
Thou by some other shalt be laid as low.
Nor think, to dye dejects my lofty Mind:
145   All that I dread, is leaving you behind!
Rather than so, ah let me still survive,
And still burn on, in *Cupid's* Flames, *Alive*.

    Restore the Locke! she cries; and all around
Restore the Locke! the vaulted Roofs rebound.
150   Not fierce *Othello* in so loud a Strain
Roar'd for the Handkerchief that caus'd his Pain.
But see! how oft Ambitious Aims are cross'd,
And Chiefs contend 'till all the Prize is lost!
The Locke, obtain'd with Guilt, and kept with Pain,
155   In ev'ry place is sought, but sought in vain:
With such a Prize no Mortal must be blest,
So Heav'n decrees! with Heav'n who can contest?

    Some thought, it mounted to the Lunar Sphere,
Since all that Man e'er lost, is treasur'd there.
160   There Heroe's Wits are kept in pondrous Vases,
And Beau's in *Snuff-boxes* and *Tweezer-Cases*.
There broken Vows, and Death-bed Alms are found,
And Lovers Hearts with Ends of Riband bound;
The Courtiers Promises, and Sick Man's Pray'rs,
165   The Smiles of Harlots, and the Tears of Heirs,
Cages for Gnats, and Chains to Yoak a Flea;
Dry'd Butterflies, and Tomes of Casuistry.

    But trust the Muse – she saw it upward rise,
Tho' mark'd by none but quick Poetic Eyes;
170   (Thus *Rome's* great Founder to the Heav'ns withdrew,
To *Proculus* alone confess'd in view.)

A sudden Star, it shot thro' liquid Air,
And drew behind a radiant *Trail of Hair*.
Not *Berenice's* Locks first rose so bright,
175   The Skies bespangling with dishevel'd Light.
This, the *Beau-monde* shall from the *Mall* survey,
As thro' the Moon-light shade they nightly stray,
And hail with Musick its propitious Ray.
This *Partridge* soon shall view in cloudless Skies,
180   When next he looks thro' *Galilæo's* Eyes;
And hence th'Egregious Wizard shall foredoom
The Fate of *Louis*, and the Fall of *Rome*.

    Then cease, bright Nymph! to mourn the ravish'd Hair,
Which adds new Glory to the shining Sphere!
185   Not all the Tresses that fair Head can boast,
Shall draw such Envy as the Locke you lost.
For, after all the Murders of your Eye,
When, after Millions slain, your self shall die;
When those fair Suns shall sett, as sett they must,
190   And all those Tresses shall be laid in Dust;
This Locke, the Muse shall consecrate to Fame,
And mid'st the Stars inscribe *Belinda's* Name!

        FINIS

Appendix 3

Pope's first translation of Sarpedon's battle speech was published as early as 1709. He made only minor changes when, years later, he incorporated the passage into his translation of the *Iliad*. It is this speech which Clarissa's advice in Canto V mocks and emulates.

Sarpedon to Glaucus

Why boast we, *Glaucus*, our extended Reign
Where *Xanthus'* Streams enrich the *Lycian* Plain?
Our num'rous Herds that range each fruitful Field,
And Hills where Vines their Purple Harvest yield?
5 Our foaming Bowls with gen'rous *Nectar* crown'd,
Our Feasts enhanc'd with Musick's sprightly Sound?
Why on these Shores are we with Joy survey'd,
Admir'd as Heroes, and as Gods obey'd?
Unless great Acts superior Merit prove,
10 And Vindicate the bounteous Powr's above:
'Tis ours, the Dignity They give, to grace;
The first in Valour, as the first in Place:
That while with wondring Eyes our Martial Bands
Behold our Deeds transcending our Commands,
15 Such, they may cry, deserve the Sov'reign State,
Whom those that Envy dare not Imitate!
Cou'd all our Care elude the greedy Grave,
Which claims no less the Fearful than the Brave,
For Lust of Fame I shou'd not vainly dare
20 In fighting Fields, nor urge thy Soul to War.
But since, alas, ignoble Age must come,
Disease, and Death's inexorable doom;
The Life which others pay, let Us bestow,
And give to Fame what we to Nature owe;
25 Brave, tho' we fall; and honour'd, if we live;
Or let us Glory gain, or Glory give!